Rachel's Secret

Rachel's Secret

SHELLY SANDERS

Second Story Press

Library and Archives Canada Cataloguing in Publication

Sanders, Shelly, 1964-
Rachel's secret / Shelly Sanders.

Issued also in electronic format.
ISBN 978-1-926920-37-5

I. Title.

PS8637.A5389R33 2012 jC813'.6 C2011-908650-6

Editor: Malcolm Lester
Line and Copy Editors: Kathryn White, Katie Todd
Design: Melissa Kaita
Cover photo © iStockphoto

Printed and bound in Canada

Second Story Press gratefully acknowledges the support of the Ontario Arts Council and the Canada Council for the Arts for our publishing program. We acknowledge the financial support of the Government of Canada through the Canada Book Fund.

ONTARIO ARTS COUNCIL
CONSEIL DES ARTS DE L'ONTARIO

Canada Council for the Arts
Conseil des Arts du Canada

Published by
Second Story Press
20 Maud Street, Suite 401
Toronto, ON M5V 2M5
www.secondstorypress.ca

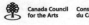

Proceed thence to the ruins, the split walls reach,
Where wider grows the hollow, and greater grows the breach;
Pass over the shattered hearth, attain the broken wall
Whose burnt and barren brick, whose charred stones reveal
The open mouths of such wounds, that no mending
Shall ever mend, nor healing ever heal . . .

—excerpt from *In the City of Slaughter*,
Hayyim Nahman Bialik

In memory of my late grandmother,
Shelly Talan Geary, to honor her courage and strength.

For all people who suffer from prejudice and discrimination.

FEBRUARY

Jewish doctors have formed a secret syndicate to swindle and defraud their unsuspecting patients through charlatanism and quackery.

—Bessarabetz, *February 11, 1903*

One

By the time Rachel saw the branch on the ice it was too late. Her skate blades had caught in the bough, throwing her off balance. She waved her arms to stay upright, but gravity pulled her over. She landed facedown on the frozen River Byk, her long black skirt flying up to her knees, revealing skinny legs in dark woolen tights.

Rachel's face flushed beet-red with embarrassment over her fall and the public display of her legs. She hastily pushed herself up and brushed the ice off her mittens and shawl.

"What happened?" Mikhail, asked as his lanky frame approached her. "One minute you were talking to me and the next minute you were down."

"Ech...a branch got in my way," she replied with a grimace. "I should have been paying more attention." She looked ahead, squinting to find her friends, but all she saw was a group of children with their parents. "Where are Chaia and Leah?"

"They're up ahead, skating with Yoram and Meyer."

Rachel shook her head and let out a long, exaggerated sigh. "Then I don't want to skate with them. Chaia acts silly around Yoram, as if he's the most important person in the world." She continued skating with Mikhail by her side, looming over her like a shadow. "But he's just the same old Yoram."

"Do you think Chaia's thinking about marriage?" Mikhail asked, running his hand though his short, white-blond hair.

"I should hope not. She…I mean *we're* far too young to be so serious." She looked away so Mikhail wouldn't see the fear in her eyes. Over the last few weeks, Leah and Chaia had been spending far more time with Yoram and Meyer than with her.

Through the barren trees clutching the edge of the narrow river, she saw the lower section of Kishinev, with its cramped wooden shanties and skeletal birches asleep for the winter. Thin, swirling lines of smoke rose from the chimneys. Rachel inhaled the flat, burnt fumes.

"My mother married when she was sixteen," said Mikhail, smiling mischievously and fixing his eyes on Rachel. "My grandmother was even younger."

Rachel noticed that the skin surrounding Mikhail's eyes creased when he smiled. "I'm not getting married until I'm a famous writer who has traveled everywhere, and I shall *only* marry if I find someone I love more than anyone else." She lengthened her stride to keep up with Mikhail, a difficult task with the afternoon wind picking up and her rusty skate blades too long for her feet. Every time she moved forward, her felt boots almost came off the blades entirely.

Mikhail's eyebrows arched. "Don't you think that's a little too much to expect? I've never heard of a woman writer…

women can't even travel without permission from their father or husband."

"There is Elena Gan, Karolina Pavlova and Isabella Grinevskaya." Rachel's eyes flashed with defiance. "Women are just as capable as men at writing. It doesn't require strength or size like you need for farming or factory work."

"But how can you be a wife, and a mother, *and* a writer?"

Rachel pressed her lips together and thought about Cecily, the rich heroine in her favorite book, *A Double Life*, by Karolina Pavlova. Cecily, trapped in a meaningless marriage, is despondent about her future, even when she sleeps and dreams:

Hold back your passion, stifle its sounds,
Teach your tears not to flow.
You are a woman! Live without defenses,
Without caprice, without will, without hope.

Even though Cecily has money, she is miserable because she has no purpose other than serving her husband. Rachel would rather be alone, writing and traveling, than be married to someone who didn't encourage her to follow her dreams. "How can *you* be a husband, a father, and work in your grandfather's business?"

Mikhail's eyes clouded over. "It's always been that way... men work and women raise the children and manage the house."

"Not me," said Rachel with shaky pride. "I don't want to end up miserable like..." She searched her memory for a character that Mikhail would know. *A Double Life* was much more popular with girls than boys. "Like Anna Karenina."

"I should hope not." Mikhail stopped skating and gave

Rachel an incredulous look. "Anna Karenina left her husband and chased after another man."

Rachel's green eyes narrowed. "She wasn't happy with her husband, so why should she stay with him?"

"Because—"

"She married the wrong person and couldn't be with the man she truly loved."

"Yes, but—"

"Everyone treated her badly, even her friends, when all she wanted was to be happy." Rachel put her hands on her hips and braced herself for another heated debate with Mikhail, their third in as many weeks.

But Mikhail's face softened, and he looked at her with a tenderness that startled Rachel. Before she knew what was happening, he had wrapped his arms around her tiny waist. Shivers ran up and down her spine. She could smell the mint on his breath and tobacco smoke on his overcoat. Feeling constrained by his arms, she tried to pull away.

He tightened his grasp, bent his head down, and kissed her for the first time.

"Stop," she cried, pushing him away. "You shouldn't have done that."

"Why not?" he demanded. "Chaia and Leah have probably already kissed Yoram and Meyer."

Rachel swallowed a lump that had suddenly lodged in her throat. "I'm not like Chaia and Leah. All they talk about is getting married and having houses of their own." She paused. "Besides, they're Jewish, Yoram and Meyer."

Mikhail frowned. "It was only a kiss. I didn't say anything about marriage."

"I know," snapped Rachel. "But if people saw us..." She turned around to see if anybody had been watching and winced when she saw Sergei, a friend of Mikhail's, approaching them.

"Have you seen Petya or Nikolai?" Sergei asked. Although he was fourteen, like Mikhail, Sergei's voice was deeper and dark hair was beginning to show above his lips.

"No, I didn't know they were here today," answered Mikhail.

Sergei turned and stared into the distance. "They must be way down the river. Too far to go now."

Rachel wished Sergei would just leave. A couple of days ago, when she had walked out of a shop with some flour to make *challah* for *Shabbos*, Sergei had bumped into her and knocked her bag out of her hands. When she saw the flour all over the ground, Rachel had looked at Sergei for an offer to buy some more. Even an apology would have been welcome. Instead, he ran off without saying a word.

"I thought we were going to race to where the river narrows, Mikhail," said Sergei.

Mikhail shrugged. "Next time. I'm skating with Rachel now."

Rachel looked away and fiddled with the tea-colored braid that hung halfway down her back.

"But you skate with Rachel every Sunday. You don't mind, do you, Rachel?"

She blinked at Sergei. "It's up to Mikhail. *I* would never force him to skate with me."

"I skate with *you* every Saturday, Sergei," Mikhail said. "I told you, I'm skating with Rachel today."

Rachel looked at Sergei and smiled—a gloating smile that she couldn't hide.

Sergei shook his head and frowned as he skated back to the river's edge, his arms flying wildly from side to side.

Rachel and Mikhail watched as Sergei sat down on the rickety wooden bench he and Mikhail had made earlier in the season. He unbuckled his skate blades and stomped away from the river.

"Why is he so angry?" she asked. Mikhail shrugged and took off across the ice. Rachel moved quickly to keep up with him, shoving Sergei and his foul temper to the back of her mind. In a way, she was grateful to Sergei for easing the tension between Mikhail and her. She wanted to forget about their kiss, pretend it had never happened.

Up ahead, Rachel saw her older sister, Nucia, showing off by skating on one leg, the other extended behind her. Tall and graceful, she looked as if she were flying on the ice.

"You're so lucky you don't have any brothers or sisters." Rachel's eyes were pasted on Nucia.

"I wouldn't mind a brother," Mikhail replied. "It's pretty quiet with just my grandparents and me."

"You may think you want a brother, but trust me, you don't…especially if your brother was better than you at everything. I hate it when Mother tells me I need to be quieter *like Nucia,* or neater *like Nucia.*" She paused to catch her breath. "Chaia has an older sister who is a very good cook. She bakes bread that melts in your mouth. So Chaia's mother expects her to be just like her sister, only Chaia can hardly make tea! If I was starving and there was no other food then maybe I'd eat Chaia's rock-hard bread. I feel sorry for her future husband. He'll probably starve to death…"

She glanced to her right and saw Mikhail's mouth twitch with amusement.

"First one to that tree leaning over the river wins," he said.

Rachel laughed and began skating faster. It took two of her strides to make one of his, and she had to keep pushing her long, bulky skirt out of the way. Mikhail was at least more than a body length ahead of her. "Just you wait, Mikhail," she called out, clutching her shawl around her. "I'm not stopping until I get you."

As soon as the words flew out of her mouth, Mikhail fell onto his back and stopped moving.

Rachel rushed over, blanketing his body with her shadow, a stricken expression on her face. As she leaned closer, Mikhail suddenly opened his eyes and grinned, his teeth glistening in the late afternoon light. Rachel fell backwards until she was sitting down on the cold ice. "I can't believe you tricked me like that," she laughed.

"I can't believe you fell for it." He got to his feet, extended his hand to help her up, and pulled her into an embrace.

"What are you doing?" she cried, squirming out of his arms. "I told you…I don't want to be with you like that."

Mikhail's jaw clenched and he eyed her with derision. "You're crazy for thinking you can choose your destiny. You will never leave Kishinev, and you will never become a writer."

Nucia's shrill voice pierced the air above the quiet river, now almost deserted. "Rachel, it's time to go," she called in Yiddish, the language Jewish families used among themselves.

Rachel heard her sister but was too upset to respond. She truly had thought that Mikhail, of all people, would understand and support her dreams, not rip through them with sharp, cynical words.

"Quickly. Mother will be angry if we're not home to help

with supper." Nucia stood on the riverbank with her arms crossed, waiting for Rachel. A couple of parents and children were also leaving the river, skates in hand.

Without a word, Rachel skated over to the bench where she slowly undid her skates, buckled them together, and stood up. She looked back and saw Mikhail skating off, away from the river's edge. Nobody else was in sight. In the distance, she heard the train whistle announcing its departure for Odessa, a sound that reminded Rachel of the larger world she desperately wanted to explore.

With a heavy heart, she walked silently beside Nucia from the river to the narrow, meandering street that led to their home.

❄❄❄

Sergei kicked the snow as he walked from the tree-lined edge of the River Byk along the muddy street that led to town. He shivered as the cold penetrated his worn leather boots and quickened his pace. Laughter erupted as he neared the ice hill where children were climbing the wooden stairs. He watched some young boys fly down the icy slide on sleds painted brightly with flowers and birds. Just a few winters ago he had spent his free time on this hill, racing Mikhail to see who could get the most slides in one afternoon.

As he continued downhill toward the crowded Jewish district, the wind smacked against his face, stinging his eyes. Uneven stones and tiles jutted out from filthy snow, and short, half-dead birch trees stooped over like old Jewish men. Sergei wrinkled his nose at the strange odors emanating from the stone walls that obscured Jewish communities along the narrow road.

He glanced through the arched gates of one courtyard. Inside were wooden houses with sagging tile roofs and a small child who looked at Sergei with mournful eyes.

The sharp whistle in the distance announced the departure of the afternoon train to Odessa. One day, Sergei promised himself, he would be on the train going somewhere, anywhere, to get away from Kishinev. He walked past the Jewish orphanage, a large, stone building with dark, narrow windows that had frightened Sergei when he was younger. His father told him that if he were really bad, he would be locked in the Jewish orphanage as a punishment. Looking at it now, Sergei decided it still looked ominous.

Sergei began walking uphill, crossing over to Aleksandrov Street and upper Kishinev, with its wide, paved sidewalks, stone office buildings, and schools, theaters, and churches. Stores, built from white stone, had red-trimmed windows, but many of them had gone out of business recently and were boarded up.

From the top of the hill, Sergei could see the whole city, set upon hilly plains. White limestone cathedrals rose up from the snow-covered evergreens, with cupolas that looked like helmets or onions. In the distance were flat steppes on which crops of sugar beets, sunflowers, wheat, maize, tobacco, and grapes would appear in the spring.

"Sergei! Wait for me!"

Turning, he saw Petya running to catch up with him. Sergei frowned. "I was looking for you on the river today."

Petya held his battered skate blades in his hands. His face was bright red from the cold—almost the color of his copper-red hair.

"Theodore, Nikolai, and I were racing at the other end of

the river," Petya replied, breathing heavily. "There were too many people in the middle. You should've come with us."

"I wish I had. Mikhail went off with Rachel, so I left." Sergei lit a cigarette with a birch splinter and they continued walking, leaving a trail of smoke behind them.

A large horse-drawn *troika* bearing a fur-clad woman and a young girl drove past. The girl wore a red hood with a deep cape and a long white cloak. The sleigh was low and small, with just enough room for two passengers and the coachman. His tall, black hat reminded Sergei of a stovepipe.

Sergei and Petya watched the troika go by, and continued on past The Moscow, where the bitter smell of beer and stale tobacco smoke hung in the air. A couple of infantry officers in green uniforms with high, stiff feathers in their caps stood outside the door, talking loudly and smoking.

"I don't understand why Mikhail skates with Rachel *every* week," said Sergei.

"Maybe because she's kind of pretty and laughs a lot." Petya pulled his collar up higher around his neck. "Do Mikhail's grandparents know he spends so much time with her?"

"He's never said."

"My father would *kill* me if I took up with a Jewish girl," said Petya, shaking his head. "We have lots of Jewish friends, like our neighbors, but my father pretends he doesn't know them if he sees them in the square. He says people complain to him, because he's the mayor, about how crowded Kishinev is becoming from all the Jews."

Sergei frowned. "My father says Jews are taking away all our jobs, that Kishinev is going to be controlled by Jews if we don't watch out."

Petya shrugged. "They do good work; my mother buys all of our shoes from a Jewish shop."

"Pretty soon there won't be anything but Jewish shops here," Sergei said. "That's why we have to make sure Jews know their place."

He and Petya walked in silence, heads down to avoid the cold wind cutting into their faces. On the corner where they went their separate ways, a tea seller was closing up for the night. The light from the gas lamps made his silver *samovar* shine.

Sergei could hardly feel his fingers by the time he arrived home, the second floor of a four-story building divided into flats. Hot air from the stove and the aroma of salted pork enveloped him when he opened the door. He removed his boots and hung his coat on an iron hook in the vestibule, then he crossed himself in front of the icon of the Madonna and infant Jesus that hung on the wall beside the door.

"Good heavens, Sergei, it's almost dark," exclaimed his mother, rushing over to him.

"I didn't realize it was so late." Sergei smiled down at her.

"Carlotta, would you come and stir the soup?" his mother asked her sister, who lived with them.

From a dimly lit corner, Carlotta emerged with a child-like smile on her plain face. Her long, gray-streaked hair hung in a loose braid down the back of her dress, which fit snugly over her podgy belly. Taking the spoon, she began humming an indecipherable melody.

"Come," said Sergei's mother, pushing him toward the fire. "Get your wet clothes off, put them by the stove, and have some tea. Make haste, before you catch a cold."

"Stop fussing over the boy," ordered Sergei's father in a

voice that resonated throughout the room. Sitting on the chintz-covered sofa, he inhaled his cigarette, filling a ceramic dish with ashes, and read the *Bessarabetz*, the local daily newspaper. As his father stroked his chin, Sergei smiled, thinking about how his friends called his father "The Beard" because his whiskers were so long.

Sergei's mother poured a glass of tea from the copper samovar. Sergei put a beetroot sugar cube in his mouth and took a sip. He savored the bitter tea as it passed through the sugar. Feeling warmer instantly, Sergei cupped his hands around the warm glass.

"When will Papa be home, Tonia?" Carlotta asked as she stirred a pot of hot cucumber soup.

Sergei's mother gently took the spoon from Carlotta. "You know that Papa is gone, Carlotta."

"Gone!" cried Carlotta. She pulled a handkerchief from her sleeve and cried into it. "The tongue speaks but the head doesn't know," she said through her tears.

Sergei's mother sighed and did what she always did when her sister had an outburst. She put her arm around her and led Carlotta to a rocking chair by the table. Then, wrapping her distraught sister in a shawl, she asked Sergei where he had been.

"I was skating with Mikhail on the river."

"Can I come next time?" asked Natalya, Sergei's eight-year-old sister. She was curled up on a chair in the corner playing with her wooden doll. A kerchief partially covered Natalya's long, black hair. Her eyes, nose, and mouth were so delicate, they looked as if they'd been drawn on her face.

"Natalya, you're too young to be out skating with your brother on the river. Anyway, there's enough around here to keep you busy," said Sergei's mother. "Now go and get the lace tablecloth from the trunk and lay it on the table. And Sergei, when you've finished your tea, put another log into the stove."

Sergei shrugged his shoulders at Natalya, who made a face when told she couldn't go skating. He took a birch log from the wood box by the door and fed the tall, black stove in the middle of the room.

"I'm famished," he said. "When will supper be ready?"

"If you're so anxious to eat, pray for patience," said his father, his face riveted to his newspaper.

"Glory hallelujah!" exclaimed Carlotta suddenly and loudly.

Sergei bit down on his bottom lip to keep from laughing.

Sergei's father turned and glared at Carlotta. "Tell your sister to be quiet," he ordered his wife.

Sergei watched as his mother cowered under his father's disapproval. He took one last sip of tea and walked over to the eastern wall of the flat where religious icons from many generations of his family hung, softly illuminated by the oil lamp. He liked the icon with the yellow background, which reminded him of the sun, even on dark days.

"Come everyone," called his mother. "It's time to eat."

Carlotta stood up, filled the bowls with soup and carried them to the table. She sat down in her spot and bent her head in prayer.

Sergei's father got to his feet, patting his ample stomach with one hand and rubbing his stiff lower back with the other. "Ah. All day I've been thinking of this food." He sat down heavily in his chair across from Sergei, Carlotta, and Natalya.

"Here it is," said Sergei's mother, bringing to the table a wooden platter filled with boiled pork, followed by a plate piled high with rye bread. She tied her apron and sat beside her husband.

Sergei's father folded his hands in prayer. "We thank thee for the food you have so graciously provided. Amen," he said.

"Amen," proclaimed Carlotta, as if she was addressing a crowd.

Sergei exchanged a smile with Natalya and began loading his plate with the boiled pork.

"Papa, Sergei is taking so much food. There won't be any left for us," Natalya whined.

"He's a growing boy, almost a man. Soon he'll become a police officer like I am." He beamed at his son. "And in a few years he'll get married and have his own family to clothe and feed."

Sergei almost choked on his meat as his father spoke. He didn't want to be a police officer, and he certainly didn't want to get married soon. Tomorrow, he vowed, he'd tell Mikhail that they had to leave soon, before his father stuck him in a uniform.

Two

Mikhail skated toward the bend in the river and thrust his face into the wind, not yet ready to go home. He wanted to clear his head, but he couldn't stop thinking about what Rachel had said, how they could never be together...yet he wanted her more than any other girl. It frustrated him, wanting something he could not have.

He pumped his legs until he was skating briskly against the wind. He loved moving fast; it made him feel free, like the fish underneath the ice. No cares or responsibilities, no grandparents expecting him to live the life they had chosen. Mikhail's brow wrinkled into folds of annoyance when he recalled the disagreement he'd had with his grandfather earlier that day.

"You must start working at the factory soon," his grandfather had said over their midday meal of bread, fish, and soup. "To gain the workers' respect, you must learn the business from the bottom up."

Mikhail had kept his eyes on his carrot soup, hoping the conversation was over. But his grandfather was persistent. His old hand, with swollen finger joints and veins that crossed his skin like lines on a map, grabbed Mikhail's wrist. Mikhail lifted his eyes and looked at his grandfather. In the background, he heard his grandmother washing pots noisily, as though reminding them that she was there.

"I'm not ready yet," Mikhail began in a cautious tone. "I want to do some other things first."

"Other things?" His grandfather stared into Mikhail's eyes.

"I…I want to travel, maybe attend university—"

"Nonsense!" His grandfather let go of Mikhail's hand and pounded his fist on the table. "How will you eat? How will you live?" His voice rose to a thundering boom. "This is nothing but a childish fairy tale. It is time to grow up!"

"I can find work," Mikhail had said, determined to change his grandfather's mind. "There is work in big cities like Petersburg."

"Please stop," his grandmother had cried, dropping her cloth into the basin. "I don't like to hear you arguing."

"But this is the only way to get some sense into this stupid boy," his grandfather had replied with obvious scorn. "Do you hear what he is planning…to travel thousands of *versts* away when he has all he needs right here?"

"Maybe this *isn't* what I need," said Mikhail, his stomach knotted with frustration. "Maybe I'm different from you…"

"Different?" scoffed his grandfather. He leaned toward his grandson until Mikhail could smell the tobacco on his breath; tobacco his grandfather's business had processed, tobacco his grandfather wanted him to process. "You are no different than

I. No different than your father who worked with pride in the business."

Mikhail groaned. His grandfather stoked his guilt by mentioning his father who, along with his mother, had been killed years ago in an accident.

"You must honor your father, do as he would have wished," his grandfather continued, his blue eyes focused on Mikhail.

"How do you know what he would have wanted?" Mikhail swallowed and had tried to think of something else to say, but his mind was blank. He had no compelling reason to avoid working with his grandfather, other than the fact that he didn't want to, which clearly was not good enough. Mikhail had left for the river without another word, but the wrath of his grandfather had been with him all afternoon, like a bad taste in his mouth.

Mikhail slowed down to catch his breath and give his burning thigh muscles a rest. He turned around and skated slowly, enjoying the view of the trees hugging the riverbank. The sun was low in the sky, yet still bright enough to make the untouched snow sparkle like sugar. His mouth watered as he thought about the sweet pastry his grandmother was making for supper. Then he thought about his grandfather and felt the anticipation drain from his body. Mikhail didn't like his grandfather being angry with him; it made everything else seem unbalanced and wrong. As he rounded the bend, he felt the hairs on his neck rise and wondered if the temperature had fallen. In the dim light, he saw two people standing near the bench.

"Uncle?" he said, when he came closer and saw his Uncle Vasily and his cousin Philip. Vasily looked bulky with a sheepskin coat over his police uniform. His thick, dirty fingers held a half-finished cigarette. Philip stood close to his father with a blank expression on his pasty face.

Though Vasily and Philip were family, they were not welcome in his grandfather's home. Something had happened before Mikhail was born, an argument that had never been resolved. Mikhail only saw his uncle and cousin in passing, usually from a distance. He'd never seen them skating.

"What are you doing here?" Mikhail skated closer and stopped when he saw his uncle's dark eyes and bitter expression.

"We came to see you," his uncle answered without smiling.

"Well...I'm just about to go home," Mikhail said shakily. He skated toward the bench to remove his blades, but his uncle blocked his way.

"Looks like you won't be going into the family business after all." An ugly sneer spread over Vasily's face.

Mikhail smelled alcohol on his uncle's breath and looked at his cousin for help. But Philip stood, legs planted firmly, mocking him in silence.

"What...what do you mean?" Mikhail stammered.

Vasily slowly exhaled his cigarette smoke directly in Mikhail's face. "I lost my position yesterday. Relieved of my duties. Poor conduct, whatever that means." He threw his cigarette on the ground. "How am I going to put food on the table?"

Mikhail cringed. "I don't know...perhaps Grandfather—"

"Ha!" Vasily spat on the ice. "He will give me nothing." His voice rose with every word. "His own son, flesh and blood. Nothing! But you...you get everything."

Mikhail started to back away but Philip thrust his leg behind his cousin's knees. Mikhail stuck his arms out to keep his balance, but fell backwards. His skull sounded like a heavy rock as it hit the ice.

Flat on his back, Mikhail didn't move for almost a minute. Then he felt his head thumping, as if it were being kicked from the inside. He opened his eyes and saw his uncle's face spinning in front of him. Everything was swirling, the trees, the sky, his cousin's eyes that seemed to come at him from every angle. Mikhail groaned and brought his hands to his head. "What... what do you want from me?" He pushed himself up with one hand so that he was sitting on the frozen river.

"I want what's coming to me," growled Vasily, planted over Mikhail like a massive tree trunk.

"I can talk to Grandfather," Mikhail offered in a weak voice. "I'm sure he'll help if you just tell him—"

"Tell him what?" Vasily's voice grew louder. "That his own son has struggled for years on a policeman's wage, and now I don't even have that?" He stepped forward, closer to Mikhail. "Your grandfather doesn't care about me or Philip. Only you. But if you're gone, he has nobody else but me to take over the business."

Mikhail turned his head to see if anyone else was nearby, but the world started spinning again. He thought he saw something red in the distance, but wasn't sure. The river was disturbingly quiet and still.

"Let me talk to Grandfather," pleaded Mikhail, still clutching his head with one hand. "I don't even want to be a tobacco processor...he'll listen to me..."

Vasily shook his head. He scowled and calmly pulled a large knife out of his coat pocket.

Unable to pry his eyes from the knife, Mikhail tried to

stand on his skates, but the blood rushing from his head made him feel dizzy and weak. He collapsed forward, onto his chest.

"Please, Philip, for once in your life, stand up to your father. Don't let him do this," Mikhail cried, pushing himself away with his hands. "I'll give you money...whatever you want."

Philip stared at him with indifference and said nothing. Vasily crouched down beside Mikhail, holding the knife in front of him.

"No!" cried Mikhail. "Uncle, please don't. Philip...help me!" He tried swiveling to his side, so he could kick his uncle with his skate blades, but Vasily was quick, despite his bulk. In one swift motion, he lifted Mikhail by his coat and stabbed him in the chest. Mikhail fell to the ground clutching his wound. His chest felt like it was on fire, burning with each breath he took.

Mikhail curled up into a ball and tried to scream when he felt the knife cutting his back, arms, and legs, but no sound came out. A scorching sensation ran down his spine. Blood filled his mouth making it difficult to breathe. Mikhail closed his eyes, clutching the silver icon that hung from a chain around his neck. He pictured his grandmother waiting for him to come home, her face pinched with worry, and his grandfather's eyes, clouded over from the horrible things Mikhail had said to him in the heat of the moment, words he would never be able to take back, words that would darken the remainder of his grandfather's days.

Remorse crushed Mikhail's heart, drained it of hope and life until his grandparents' faces became blurry, then disappeared. Mikhail felt himself gliding forward to a shadowy abyss, and then his pain was gone.

❄❄❄

"Oh no! I don't have my shawl," Rachel cried to Nucia when they were halfway home. "I must have dropped it somewhere." Rachel stopped and stared at her sister.

"Your new red shawl, the one Mother knitted for your birthday?"

Rachel gulped. "Yes."

Nucia shook her head and folded her arms across her chest. "You must go back for it. Mother will be *very* angry if you lose it. She spent *hours* working on it."

Just once, Rachel thought, couldn't Nucia be the one to forget something? "But it's going to be dark soon."

"Then you had better run," Nucia said.

Rachel turned and fled back toward the river, the cold air drying her throat, making it hard to catch her breath. She saw her shawl not far from the bench, on the ground behind a dense stand of fir trees. As she bent down to pick it up, Rachel heard a familiar voice crying out for help. She froze. Another voice, deep and muffled, was speaking, but she couldn't make out what was being said. She crept toward a small opening in the trees, peered through the prickly branches, and gasped. Mikhail was lying on the ice underneath two other people, heavy-set men she did not recognize. The bigger man, wearing a sheepskin coat and a policeman's distinctive cap, held a long knife.

"Uncle, please don't do this," cried Mikhail. "Philip, help me."

Rachel clamped her hands over her mouth. *His uncle? How could that be?* She watched the policeman bend down, lift Mikhail as easily as a rag doll, and plunge the knife into his chest in one quick movement. Mikhail clutched his abdomen and barely whimpered when the knife cut into his back again and again.

Rachel turned and ran, shawl in hand. Her feet smashed down on the snow and she flinched as she heard the crunch of dead branches and leaves under her feet. She tripped over a tree root and fell on her face.

"Who's there?"

Her insides twisted into a knot as the threatening voice came closer and closer. Mikhail's uncle knew someone had witnessed the stabbing. Without stopping to wipe the muddy snow from her skirt and legs, Rachel scrambled to her feet and ran. She could hear footsteps behind her, but raced ahead without looking back until the footsteps grew fainter and receded into the distance. Her face was wet with perspiration and tears. Only when she saw the peeling walls that surrounded her house did Rachel slow down to catch her breath.

Once she'd entered the gate and was safely in her courtyard, Rachel was relieved to find that everyone, including old Mr. Gervitz, who sat outside regularly since losing his job, had gone inside. She rushed to one of the outhouses in the corner of the courtyard where she could be alone. "Mikhail, oh Mikhail," she whispered, shutting the rickety door behind her. Tears fell onto her dirty skirt and guilt turned her heart inside out as she recalled kissing him. Rachel feared that Mikhail's uncle had seen them together, that maybe she was partly to blame for the stabbing.

She wiped her eyes and tried to quiet her breathing, as if she could will away the horror. But the sound of Mikhail's screams and the sight of his uncle looming over him with a knife were seared into her brain.

Rachel fervently regretted her anger toward Mikhail when they had parted. If only Mikhail hadn't kissed her, then she wouldn't have been mad and he might still be alive. Now he was dead, and she couldn't even go to the police to seek justice... because the murderer was a policeman! A sense of doom and profound despair settled in her chest.

Rachel tried to tidy her hair and skirt and opened the door of the outhouse. It was a cold, still night, a perfect night for sitting by the fire and playing chess with her father; a perfect night for wrapping herself in a warm blanket and listening to her father play his violin. But the peacefulness was deceiving, thought Rachel as she traipsed to the door. Beneath the silence was a nightmare so real, it chilled her to the core. She didn't think she would ever feel warm again, or safe, or content.

"Look at you!" cried her mother, dropping the spoon she was holding when Rachel entered. She wiped her pale hands on her apron and bent down to pick up the spoon. "I thought you were going to fetch your shawl, yes?"

Rachel glanced down at her empty hands and realized she must have dropped the shawl when she was running away from the river. She began twirling her braid nervously and looked away from her mother to the steaming samovar on the stove.

"And your skirt? Do you know how much work it is to wash your clothes?"

"I'm sorry, Mother, I...fell," said Rachel, casting her gaze at the floor. The smell of cabbage soup was making her nauseous.

"Why can't you take care of your things, like your sister?"

Nucia, who was getting bowls out of the cupboard, smirked at Rachel. Ordinarily, Rachel would have glared at her sister, but now she ignored her, giving her mother a vague shrug.

"Let her catch her breath." Her father stood by their only window, overlooking the courtyard, holding a glass of tea. "Are you all right, Rachel?"

"Yes…I just…well…I never made it to the river." Her swollen eyes darted from her father to her mother.

"Where were you then?" asked her mother.

"I was…running…so I could get my shawl and come home, but I…I tripped over a tree root and fell down a hill, which is why I'm so dirty." She paused to think up the next part of her lie. "The sky was getting dark and the…the trees started to look like skeletons, and the wind was howling so loudly, making sounds I'd never heard before and…I think a brown bear was nearby…I was frightened and ran home before I could find my shawl."

"Ech," said her mother, shaking her head and mumbling to herself. "This girl…she doesn't appreciate what I do for her. After long days of cooking and cleaning, I knit her a beautiful red shawl. And what does she do? She loses it."

"Ita, stop. Leave the girl alone," said Rachel's father. He turned toward Rachel, his face dark with concern. "I've told you many times that bears only come out in the middle of the night, when we're sleeping, Rachel. They're more afraid of us than we are of them. Now go and change your clothes and come for supper."

She nodded at her father and slipped behind the muslin curtain in the corner of the room where she and Nucia slept on a wooden bench. Away from the questioning looks of her family, she let the tears she'd been fighting flow down her face. She fell onto her stomach and cried silently into her feather pillow until she was limp, a dry rag, with every tear wrung out of her.

❄❄❄

"Rachel skated with that boy again today," said Nucia, when they sat down to dinner. "Mikhail."

Rachel's heart fluttered, as if it were broken into a hundred little pieces. She moved her spoon listlessly around in her soup.

"What people must have thought when they saw you," cried Rachel's mother. She brought her hands to her bony cheeks. "We are respectable Jews, *menshe yiden*, and cannot behave in such a manner."

"Ita, calm yourself," said Rachel's father, buttering a piece of bread. "Rachel, it might not be a wise idea to spend so much time with a gentile." He put his knife down. "Why can't you be friends with a nice Jewish boy?"

Rachel looked at her father. "I'm not hungry."

"What?" Rachel's mother cried. "First she loses her shawl and now she refuses to eat perfectly good food."

Rachel caught her father's eye. He pressed his lips together and nodded at her, giving permission for her to leave the table. She backed away without looking at her mother who was still muttering under her breath.

❄❄❄

Rachel stood in front of her bed, too distraught for sleep, her eyes blinking back tears. She saw her wooden doll, the one her mother had given her years ago, standing on the shelf above her bench, and wished she could go back in time to when she was little and life was simple. With a trembling hand, Rachel picked up her doll—named Snegurochka after the snow maiden in her favorite fairy tale—and stared at the hand-painted face with its scarlet lips and turquoise eyes. Snegurochka loved Ivan, a human, and he loved her. Ivan gave up everything to live with Snegurochka in a castle made of snow because she would melt if she tried to enter his world.

Seeing Mikhail killed made Rachel wonder if their friendship was to blame, because he'd ventured outside his world and into hers, because he'd cared about her more than he should have. Without even removing her skirt, Rachel, still clutching her doll, climbed onto her bench, pulled her feather quilt over her head and rolled into a tight ball, knees to her chest. When she closed her eyes, all she saw was Mikhail on the ice, in a pool of blood as red as the shawl she'd lost.

Three

The morning passed slowly, with Sergei constantly peering at Mikhail's empty desk. In rapid French, the teacher conjugated verbs, his monotonous voice drifting incoherently into the background. Sergei began doodling on his paper.

With swift, bold strokes he drew the rectangular outline of a building he'd pictured in his head. The roof was a flat, wide triangle, and the windows were large with arches on top. As the drawing took shape, he added texture with bolder lines and shading.

"Conjugez le verbe envoyer au passé composé, Sergei. Est-ce que vous écoutez?"

Sergei looked up to see his teacher, Mr. Pollkin, scowling at him from the front of the room. Sergei's face was deep red as he stood up before his classmates.

"Je ne sais pas," he replied.

Mr. Pollkin's large, bulging eyes looked as if they were

going to pop out of his oversized head. Sergei knew his teacher demanded the full attention of his students at all times, and that he was in trouble. As he stood waiting to hear his punishment, a knock sounded at the classroom door.

"Entrez," ordered Mr. Pollkin, without taking his eyes off Sergei.

The students gasped as a police officer strode into the room, dressed in the familiar gray uniform, buttoned right up to the collar.

"It has come to our attention that a boy from this class is missing," announced the officer. "Mikhail Rybachenko went ice-skating on the River Byk yesterday and never returned home. Blood was discovered on the ice. Naturally, his grandparents are quite concerned."

Sergei froze. The officer scanned the class, which had become so quiet that Sergei could hear the wind growling outside.

Clearing his throat, the policeman asked, "Did any of you see him skating yesterday?"

Realizing that every boy's eyes were now on him—Mikhail's closest friend—Sergei stepped forward slowly.

"Come with me," the officer barked.

Sergei dragged his feet through the doorway and then followed the officer down the hall. On the way he heard a Latin class reciting verses and wished he were there, or anywhere else, and that Mikhail was with him.

They entered an empty classroom. The officer settled into a chair behind the desk. Sergei stood facing him.

"Your name," he began, holding a pen over his notebook.

"Sergei. Sergei Khanzhenkov."

The officer's eyebrows rose and he removed his spectacles. "Are you related to Chief Khanzhenkov?"

Sergei nodded. "He's my father."

The policeman pursed his lips as he mulled over this information. He put his glasses back on. "Very well. Continue."

"I saw Mikhail and this girl, Rachel, yesterday, skating on the river."

"What time was that?"

"About four o'clock, I think. I didn't look at my watch."

"What were they doing?"

"I told you...they were skating."

The officer scowled. "Don't be rude. Now, how does Mikhail know her?"

Sergei pulled at his collar, which was suddenly choking him. "We met her one day when we were skating last winter."

"Were they fighting when you left them?"

"No." Sergei clenched his teeth. He knew he should tell the officers he'd seen Mikhail kiss Rachel, but he didn't want to make trouble for Mikhail.

"Do you know where this Rachel lives? Her last name?"

"I think it's Paskar, and she lives in lower Kishinev."

The officer removed his spectacles again, stood up, and leaned over the table so that Sergei could smell his sour breath. "So she's Jewish, a Yid."

"What difference does that make?" asked Sergei.

The officer stared at him. "Do you have anything more to say?"

Sergei shook his head.

"Go back to your class then. We're through, for now."

Sergei backed out of the doorway slowly, breaking into a sweat as soon as the door closed behind him.

❄❄❄

A loud tapping persisted in Sergei's head as he slept. He tossed and turned from side to side, but the tapping was relentless, shattering his sleep. He sat up groggily and rubbed his eyes. It was still dark outside, the middle of the night.

Shivering, he left his bed and trudged out of his room to the sitting room, where the stove burned all night. His father stood in the open doorway to their flat, his back to Sergei.

"When was this?" his father was asking, his voice raspy with sleep.

A man answered his father. Sergei yawned and sat down by the stove, which gave off a comfortable warmth.

"And there was nothing on his feet, hmm?" his father continued. "I'll be there at first light."

Sergei feared the resignation in his father's voice.

His father shut the door and sighed.

"What is it, Papa?" asked Sergei.

His father jumped and turned at the sound of Sergei's voice. "Why are you up, hmm?"

"The person at the door woke me."

"Ah." His father pulled up a chair and sat beside Sergei. "I have some bad news." He paused, as if he wasn't sure of how to proceed. "A peasant has come across a body, in a garden in Dubossary."

Sergei was unable to move or speak. He knew what was coming, but didn't want to hear it.

"I think it is Mikhail."

The bile in Sergei's stomach rose to his throat. "No…no…I don't believe it!" He wanted his father to tell him it was all a mistake—that Mikhail was safe at home with his grandparents. But his father looked grim and began pouring water into the samovar to make tea.

Sergei's face turned white with shock. "No. It's not possible…it's not…Mikhail. Why would Mikhail be in Dubossary, so far from here?"

His father scratched his head. "Perhaps he was taken there by the person who killed him. We won't know until after the autopsy, but my officer says there are a number of stab wounds on the body."

Sergei's head began spinning. He felt dizzy and sick and faint. "The body; how can you refer to him as 'the body'? He's a person, my friend—" He jumped up and kicked his chair. "And he's not dead. Nobody would ever hurt Mikhail. Nobody."

His father looked at Sergei with a grave face. "A stranger may be responsible, someone who knows nothing about Mikhail…"

Sergei's eyes burned with rage. "That doesn't make any sense, it has to be a mistake; Mikhail isn't dead, he's at home with his grandparents. I know it." Before his father could respond, he ran back to his room and slammed the door.

❄❄❄

Standing near the edge of the River Byk, Sergei showed his father where he'd left Mikhail on Sunday, two days earlier. His hand shook as he pointed to the spot. Mikhail's death had now been confirmed. Sergei's emotions conflicted between a thirst for revenge, and remorse for the argument he'd had with Mikhail the last time they'd been together.

"There, where the river's the widest. That's...where he was standing the last time..." His voice was tense, "...the last time I saw him, with Rachel. There were some other people skating not far from them as well."

"How many people, hmm?"

"I don't know. Maybe seven or eight."

"Did you know any of them?"

"No."

"Were they all Jewish?"

"Why are you and the rest of the police so obsessed with the Jews?"

"I'm asking the questions. Not you."

Sergei scowled at his father and then pasted his eyes onto the river. "If only Mikhail had come with me instead of staying with Rachel."

"Don't go near that girl. Do you hear me?"

"She didn't have *anything* to do with his death," said Sergei, shouting out the words with a fierceness that surprised even him.

"How can you be so certain? Were you there?"

"They were friends, and she's half his size."

"Just do as I say and stay away from her. She's bad luck." His father reached into his waist pouch for a cigarette, lit it with a birch splinter, and inhaled. He wrote some notes on his paper, his cigarette dangling from his lips. Then he beckoned one of his officers to look at the bloody trail from the ice in front of the bench to the snow-covered ground.

Sergei turned away from his father, disappointed that he would even consider Rachel a murderer, and waded through the heavy snow on the riverbank far past the bench. The sky was gray and the birch trees sagged as if they were bent in grief. As he walked by the dormant trees that obscured his view of the river, something red on the frozen ground caught his eye. Perhaps it was a clue to Mikhail's murder, he thought as he strode toward it purposefully.

It was Rachel's shawl, the one she had been wearing when she was skating with Mikhail. Looking around to make sure nobody was watching, Sergei picked it up and stuffed it inside his bulky sheepskin coat.

❄❄❄

Rachel could hear the wind's menacing howl moaning through the cracks of the house, like heavy, deep breaths, taunting her as she tossed and turned. Mikhail stood before her with a knife plunged into his chest. Begging her for help. But she stood silently, unmoving.. Listening as his cries grew louder and louder and louder...watching as he fell to his death. Footsteps chasing her, getting closer and closer, louder and louder...

Rachel sat up, her chest heaving rapidly up and down. She threw her quilt to the floor. At the other end of the bench, Nucia slept peacefully, breathing in a steady, comfortable rhythm.

She wanted to show respect for Mikhail, just as she had honored her mother's parents when they died a year ago. Her family had sat *Shiva* for seven days. They hadn't looked in the mirror, bathed, or washed their hair for a week, and her mother even tore a piece of her skirt...Rachel sat up quickly and reached down to the bottom of her nightdress. Grabbing the cotton between her thumb and forefinger, she pulled as hard as she could, but it wouldn't tear. Feeling around for the seam, she pulled until the fabric ripped apart. Now Rachel felt like she had truly honored the separation between her and Mikhail. Now she could try to sleep.

❄❄❄

"You're awake!"

Her mother's voice startled Rachel as she poured herself a glass of tea, spilling it all over the samovar.

"How can you be so messy?" said her mother. "You must be more careful."

Fetching a rag from the water bucket, Rachel wiped the samovar clean.

"You look better. You'll go back to school tomorrow," said Rachel's mother before emptying her birch-bark basket of the tea and cabbage she had just purchased. "Idleness is the mother of all vices."

"But Mother, I still don't feel well."

"What if I didn't cook your meals or wash your clothes when I was ill? You'd starve, yes?"

Rachel frowned and headed back into her sleeping area. She needed to write about what she'd seen, to ease the burden within her heart that was becoming heavier by the minute. The pages of her journal were her friends, better than real friends, for they would not talk or reveal her secrets.

"Where are you going?" asked her mother as she lit the oil lamp sitting on the table.

"To write in my journal."

Her mother pulled out a white piece of cloth from a basket near the stove. "If you're well enough to write, you're well enough to help me. Come," she motioned with her finger. "You will embroider this challah cover."

"But—"

"Don't argue with me. Now, here's some red and blue thread. The scroll work should be in red and the flowers in blue."

For hours, it seemed to Rachel, she sat and stitched, doing her best to keep the threads even and smooth, which was almost impossible with her clumsy hands. She poked her fingers with the needle more times than she could count. Knots appeared out of nowhere, causing her to stop and cut the thread. Her head throbbed and her eyes were strained and heavy.

"You're actually doing needlework!" said Nucia when she arrived home from her work as a seamstress. "I can't believe what I'm seeing."

"Nucia, enough," said their mother as she cut a head of cabbage for soup. "She's been sitting all day working. Let her finish." She put her knife down and poured a glass of tea from the samovar. "Come, Nucia, and have some hot tea before we make dinner."

Rachel clumsily pushed the needle through the fabric and accidentally pricked her thumb. A tiny red spot appeared on her skin. The door swung open bringing a gust of cold air into the room. Rachel's father, home from his job as a shoemaker's assistant, entered with a somber expression on his weary face.

"What's wrong, Gofsha?" asked Rachel's mother.

He stomped his feet to get rid of the snow. "That boy Rachel knows—Mikhail—he was found dead in Dubossary. It was on the front page of the newspaper. Police think he was taken there after he was killed."

Rachel froze with terror. She desperately wanted to tell

her father what she'd seen but was afraid he wouldn't believe that a police officer was responsible. He might think she'd been mistaken, that it wasn't an officer at all, and insist on going to the police. Then the man who'd killed Mikhail would know she had seen him and come after her.

"When did you last see Mikhail?" her father asked.

"Sun...Sunday," she stammered. "We skated together, but when I left he was on the river."

"I was with Rachel, Father," added Nucia. "We walked away and he still had his skates on."

Rachel pressed her lips together and gave Nucia a grateful look.

Her father stroked his whiskers for a moment, then he put a log in the stove, poured himself a glass of tea, and sat down at the table with his newspaper. "Did his parents know he was friendly with you, Rachel?"

"His parents died a long time ago." Her voice faltered. "He lived with his grandparents; I don't know if he told them about me."

"I don't want you going anywhere alone for a while. And you as well, Ita. Make sure either Nucia or Rachel is with you when you go beyond lower Kishinev."

Rachel's mother put the *kugel* in the oven and looked at her husband anxiously. "Gofsha, surely you don't think we're in danger."

Rachel's father put his paper down on the table and scratched his head. "Ech. I just don't want to take any chances. There is talk that a Jew is to blame for the boy's murder, and though there's no proof, Mikhail's death has certainly added fuel to the fire."

Later, when she climbed onto her bench to go to sleep, Rachel pictured herself throwing branches on a blazing fire and shook her head to get rid of the image. She sat up for hours writing in her journal under the light from an oil lamp, while the rest of her family slept.

If only I could have stopped Mikhail's uncle, she wrote in Yiddish. *For as long as I live, I will regret my actions, my cowardice.* She stopped, dipped her pen in the inkwell and stared off into the darkness before continuing. *I regret also my friendship with Mikhail. I see now that it was wrong, that people from two different worlds do not belong together.* She blew on the page to dry the ink, closed her journal, and tried to go to sleep. But all night she twisted and turned, consumed by a flame that grew bigger and bigger in her mind until it was out of control.

Four

Rachel rubbed her eyes, underlined in half-moon shadows, and looked out the narrow window of her school, the Kishinev Jewish Gymnazyium. She watched people hurrying along the street, holding their hats to keep them from blowing away. Her head pounded. Another night of frightening sounds and visions had robbed her of much-needed sleep.

At the front of the room, Mr. Dubnow's bony hand fingered his long white beard as he announced that school was over. "Gut Shabbos my children," he called out, rising from behind his tall desk.

Rachel followed Chaia and Leah through the crowded hallway to the heavy door that led outside.

"We're staying home from *shul* tomorrow because my father doesn't think it's safe," said Chaia as they stepped onto the wooden sidewalk. Her golden hair shimmered in the daylight like neatly tied strands of wheat. "Yoram's family isn't going either."

"Neither are we," said Leah. "My father saw a stupid article in the newspaper yesterday that said Mikhail may have been killed by a Jew for his blood." She linked arms with Chaia and they moved briskly ahead of Rachel, the snow crunching beneath their feet.

"That's crazy," said Chaia.

"Yes, and there's more. The writer also said Jews have discovered a way to make wine without grapes and are going to take over the entire industry."

"You can't make wine without grapes," said Rachel, stepping quickly to keep up with her friends. "That would be like saying we're making cabbage soup without cabbage. It doesn't make any sense."

Leah smiled. "Nothing makes sense anymore—the newspaper, what people believe about us, Mikhail's death. That's why my father doesn't want us going to shul. He says we would be as vulnerable as pieces of meat on a plate, especially after Mikhail—" She stopped and looked at Rachel. "I feel terrible about what happened to him."

"So do I," said Chaia. "He was a good friend."

Tears welled up in Rachel's eyes.

"You were one of the last people to see him," Chaia continued. "Did he say anything? Was he worried about something?"

Rachel shook her head. "No." She didn't tell them about her quarrel with Mikhail. It was personal, and Chaia couldn't be trusted to keep it to herself.

Chaia linked her arm through Rachel's and the three girls walked the rest of the way in silence along the narrow, unpaved street, past shanties and crooked two-story dwellings with dingy shops on the main level and cramped flats overhead.

❄❄❄

The moment Rachel arrived home, her mother ushered her and Nucia out the door to the community *mikveh*, the bath used to purify themselves before Shabbos. Rachel and her sister undressed and waited in the outer room because someone was already inside. Only one person at a time could enter the room with the water. After a couple of minutes, Chaia's mother came out of the bath, her face red and shiny from the heat. She said hello and started to get dressed. Rachel walked into the next room and down the stairs into the hot water. When her cold skin met the heat, she shuddered until her body adjusted to the higher temperature. She closed her eyes and dipped her entire body into the fresh water. Three times for holiness.

Rachel submerged her head and wished the water could wash away the past, erase what had happened to Mikhail so that he would still be alive. When she was finished, she sat on the top step, staring at the water, until she began shivering and her pale skin broke out into little bumps.

❄❄❄

"*Sholom aleichem!*" said Mr. Talansky. "Peace be upon you."

Rachel looked up from the gefilte fish she was helping her mother stuff with eggs, onions, and pepper to see Mr. Talansky in the doorway. He was a broad man with curly brown hair and eyes that beamed when he spoke. As he marched confidently into their flat, the whole room seemed brighter. Even her mother smiled.

"Aleichem sholom," said Rachel. Mr. Talansky and his

sixteen-year-old son, Sacha, had been friends of their family for as long as Rachel could remember, spending many Shabbos evenings in their home since Mrs. Talansky had died years ago.

"Sholom aleichem, Rachel," said Sacha, his lively brown eyes focused on her. "I have a quote for you."

Funny Sacha. He always had a joke or a riddle to amuse her. His laugh reminded her of Mikhail, and how he had tricked her by falling on the ice. Rachel tried to smile, but couldn't coax her lips to move. A wave of grief and guilt swallowed her up, sucking the air out of her.

"What's the matter, Rachel?" asked her father. "You look as though you might faint." He put his arms around her waist, holding her up, until the lightheadedness passed and Rachel was able to breathe normally.

"I'm just hungry and tired," she said.

"Then we must begin Shabbos," her father announced. He guided Rachel to the table where her mother lit two white candles. They all said a prayer over wine. One by one, Rachel's family and the Talanskys washed their hands using the bucket of water near the stove. They said a blessing over the loaves of challah, which were covered with the cloth Rachel had embroidered.

The bread seemed dull and tasteless to Rachel, a dense lump she could barely swallow.

"*L'chayim*," said Rachel's father, raising his glass of wine. "May his great name be blessed forever and for all eternity. Amen."

"Amen," said everyone at once, before taking a sip of wine.

Rachel saw Sacha look hungrily at the potato kugel. She knew he didn't get to eat homemade food since his mother had died, because his father had no idea how to make a kugel or even challah.

"There's talk of riots at shul, Gofsha," said Mr. Talansky, after he finished a mouthful of kugel. "The gentile's newspaper, what's the name of it again?" He drummed on the table, then snapped his fingers. "*The Bessarabetz*. That's it. The editor there is writing all kinds of rubbish, saying Jews are parasites..."

"Ech. That's a horrible rumor," said Rachel's father, cutting off Mr. Talansky. "Not something that should be discussed at Shabbos."

Rachel stared at the table, her mind going back to the last time she had seen Mikhail, to their kiss. Any gentile would have been horrified to see one of their own kissing a Jew. Maybe these riots were being planned to punish all Jews for her terrible mistake.

❄❄❄

Sergei watched his little sister on the swing as she flew high as a bird and then sailed backwards. Before long, Natalya would be too big for the swing, he realized. Having a young child in the house had taken away some of his father's meanness, softened his hard edges. Turning from Natalya, Sergei looked all around Chuflinskii Square for his parents. He saw a long line for the colorful merry-go-round, and a group of children that had gathered to watch the jugglers and mimes. His parents had disappeared into the bustling crowd of people celebrating the last day of Butter Week. Tomorrow, Lent would begin and butter would not be allowed.

He put his hands in his pocket to touch Rachel's shawl. As

his fingers brushed over the wool, he decided that Rachel must have lost it on her way home from skating. He remembered how Mikhail had gazed at her, as if she were the only person on earth. There was no way Rachel was involved in Mikhail's murder. He was as sure of this as he was of his own innocence, and was glad that his father or another police officer hadn't found Rachel's shawl.

Sergei pulled a corner of the shawl out of his pocket and bent his face forward to inhale…a faint scent of soap and tea and cinnamon. Exactly what he had noticed when he had bumped into her in front of the shop. He cringed, thinking about how he had run off without helping her clean up the flour or even apologizing. For some reason, he wilted in her presence, felt like an idiot, and stumbled over his words.

He stuffed the shawl back in his pocket and glanced around the square to make sure nobody was looking at him. Though Sergei knew he should give the shawl back to Rachel, he liked having it in his pocket so he could touch it whenever he wanted.

"I want some something to eat. I'm hungry. Sergei, are you listening?" asked Natalya. She had finally gotten off the swing. Her pale cheeks were flushed from the cold.

"Let's go to a vendor." Sergei grabbed Natalya's small hand and together they pushed through the crowd until they found a booth selling *blini*. Sergei handed the vendor some *kopecks* and he and Natalya sat at a round outdoor table to eat.

Sergei put a forkful of the thin pancake in his mouth and savored the rich, buttery flavor. Last year, he and Mikhail had a contest to see who could eat the most. Mikhail won after stuffing thirty blini in his mouth. Sergei had stopped at twenty-six and had an awful bellyache for two days. Sergei's insides clenched uncomfortably as he thought about Mikhail. He pushed his plate away.

"I wish we could have one less week of Lent," said Natalya. "I'm going to miss butter and meat and eggs."

"Me too," said Sergei, hoping his sister didn't notice his uneaten blini. "Seven weeks of Lent feels like a whole year."

"Are you thinking about Mikhail?" asked Natalya. She'd finished her pancakes and was licking her fingers.

"Yes. I can't understand why anyone would want to hurt him."

"What's a blood ritual?"

"Where did you hear about that?" he asked in a solemn voice.

"My friend Maria. She heard her parents talking about it when they thought she was asleep. They said Jews eat blood—it's called a blood ritual. Is that true?"

"I don't think so." He bit his lip. "You shouldn't be talking about that."

"Why?"

"Because you're only eight, too young to worry about bad things."

"I'm not too young. Besides, everybody's talking about Mikhail being killed by Jews for blood. My friends, my teachers, everyone."

"Well, you and your friends should be talking about other things, like schoolwork or games."

"That's not as interesting as Mikhail. Why do you think they wanted his blood?"

"I told you, I'm not talking about Mikhail anymore." Sergei

turned away and watched people mingling in the square. A couple of young peasant men with shaggy sheepskin coats, long hair, and flowing beards were marching toward a well-dressed Jewish family, shouting, "No Yids allowed! Yids go home!"

Sergei gasped. These Jewish people had done nothing wrong. The three children began crying as they lagged behind the adults. The biggest child, a boy with long dark brown hair, put his arms around the two little girls, prodding them toward the shops on the opposite side of the square.

Sergei reached out and took Natalya's hand. Her eyes were riveted on the children.

When the peasants blocked the Jews from moving forward, the father raised his head and looked one of the men squarely in the eyes. The peasant blew cigarette smoke in the Jewish man's face. The woman kept her eyes on the ground as she adjusted her kerchief. Both peasants spat at the man's face. He didn't blink.

Sergei motioned vigorously to a shopkeeper leaning against his window. He saw the man shift his gaze toward the Jews for a second. Then he looked back at Sergei, shrugged his shoulders, and sauntered back into his store.

Disgusted by the shopkeeper's apathy, Sergei stood and told Natalya to get off her chair.

Both of the peasants were now kicking the Jewish man and woman in the shins. The cries of their children punctured the air.

"Sergei, why are the men hurting those people?" asked Natalya, who looked stricken. "Did they do something wrong?"

"No," said Sergei. "Those peasants are fools. Come. We must find Papa and bring him here to stop things before they get out of control."

Five

Mikhail skated quickly along the river. Smiling. All of a sudden, he was lying on the ice in a puddle of blood. And his eyes were open, water frozen to his lashes, like icicles dripping from the needles of an alder tree.

With a shudder, Rachel tried to put last night's dream out of her mind and forced herself to concentrate on the morning service at shul—the Synagogue of the Glaziers. She gazed up at the coffered ceiling and studied the Jewish symbols, then looked down from the women's gallery at the half-empty prayer hall and saw her father sitting tall, in spite of the threats that had kept so many other people from attending.

Rabbi Yitzchak's resonant voice echoed off the walls of the sanctuary, filling hollow spaces with the morning blessings. The familiar words, chanted in Hebrew, were soothing, but Rachel couldn't focus. Her mind drifted to the never-ending dilemma that plagued her night and day...if only she hadn't kissed Mikhail...if only she hadn't argued with him...if only she could've convinced him to go home when she left the river that day. Rachel felt a tap on her shoulder and spun around to see Nucia glaring at her for not paying attention. She nodded and turned toward Rabbi Yitzchak, but her mind stayed on Mikhail and her regrets.

After the service, Rachel traipsed home beside her father. Nucia and her mother were a few steps ahead of them. Her father was telling her what he thought of the service when an earsplitting scream sliced through the quiet morning. Rachel stopped in her tracks. She put her hands over her face and crouched down, as if to hide.

"Rachel, are you all right?" asked her father, bending down and wrapping his arms around her. "It was just some boys teasing a girl. Nobody is hurt. Look."

Rachel's eyes followed his hand, which was pointing straight ahead at a group of children laughing together.

Her father's forehead wrinkled into folds of concern. "Why are you so afraid?"

"Father," she said, "if you had a secret but knew it could cause trouble if you told, what would you do?"

He looked at her thoughtfully before answering. "That depends. Would anyone be hurt if this secret was revealed?"

Rachel imagined the police beating down her family's door to stop her from telling people what she had seen. She pictured the big policeman in the sheepskin coat chasing her through the forest, waving a bloody knife in the air as he grew closer.

"Yes," she said. "I...people could get hurt."

You know that Jewish law forbids gossip and slander—*lashon ha-ra.*"

"But when you know for sure that someone did a terrible thing..."

"Stop," her father said sternly. "Disparaging words are prohibited. Especially if your words could bring about violence."

"But Father—"

"Listen to me." He placed his hands on her shoulders. "Words that question another's character are like feathers thrown into the wind. They can never be returned."

She nodded.

"Is this secret the reason you've been acting so strangely? You haven't been eating, and every morning you have dark circles under your eyes."

Rachel wasn't sure how to answer her father. She knew he would insist on telling the police what she'd seen, but he didn't know how that policeman had stabbed Mikhail, with a vengeance and anger that truly horrified her. "Perhaps," she said slowly.

"You are a wise girl. You will know in your heart if you should reveal your secret."

They resumed walking in silence. Rachel wondered how she would know, if there would be a sign or if she would have to figure it out herself. She didn't have a chance to think about this further, for when they entered their courtyard, a young police officer was waiting at their door.

"Good day," said the policeman.

"The same to you," said Rachel's father. He glanced up at the clear blue sky and cleared his throat. "I think spring will be early this year."

The officer nodded. "I, um, don't mean to bother you and take up much of your time. It seems that your daughter Rachel was one of the last people to see Mikhail Rybachenko alive at the river. I just have a couple of questions for her."

Her father nodded. "I knew you would be here sooner or later. This is Rachel. Come in."

Rachel followed her father and the policeman inside.

"Allow me to introduce my wife, Ita," said Rachel's father, "and my older daughter, Nucia." The two of them were seated quietly near the stove, on a bench that doubled as a bed for Rachel's parents in the evening. The officer bowed his head toward them, then leaned against the wall. "Nucia was with Rachel the last time she saw Mikhail," Rachel's father added.

The officer fixed his eyes on Rachel, who had joined her mother and sister on the bench. "Can you tell me, umm, about the last few minutes you spent with Mikhail?" asked the policeman.

Rachel glanced at her father, who nodded, and began to speak. "There was nobody except Mikhail on the ice when we, Nucia and I, left the river." Rachel looked down to hide her tears. "I wish he had gone home."

"It's true," said Nucia. "When we left, Mikhail was alone."

"Do you know of anyone who wanted to hurt Mikhail? Somebody who might have been mad at him?"

Rachel shook her head and looked at the officer, her eyes brimming with tears. "Everyone liked Mikhail. He…he… always knew the right thing to say and never had a harsh word for anyone."

Rachel's father cleared his throat. "Are…are you finished?"

The policeman examined his notes. "I'm sorry to have upset you like this, but, umm, we need all the information we can get in order to find the person responsible."

❄❄❄

Mikhail's eyes stared at her, bright blue saucers in a pool of blood.

"No!" screamed Rachel. She sat up, looked around the dark sleeping area and began crying softly into her pillow.

"What's wrong, Rachel?" Nucia called out sleepily.

"Nothing." Rachel answered in a teary voice.

Nucia got up and shuffled over to her. "This is the third night in a row that you've had a nightmare. Is it about Mikhail?" She yawned as she spoke.

"I can't tell you." Rachel reached for Snegurochka and clutched the doll to her chest for comfort.

"Why not?"

Rachel looked up at her sister, a shadow against the wall. "Because I could get our whole family in trouble," she whispered.

"What are you talking about?"

Rachel sat up and pulled her blanket up to her neck. "I told you. I can't say."

"What if I promise not to tell anybody?"

"How can I trust *you*?"

"You know that amber necklace Mother gave me last year? The one she's had since she was a girl?"

Rachel nodded.

"I'll give it to you for safekeeping. If I break my promise, it's yours."

Rachel closed her eyes for a moment and considered her sister's offer. Entrusting her secret would be like sharing a burden, sharing the fear. "I saw something, something horrible that nobody was supposed to see."

"What?" asked Nucia, now wide awake.

Rachel took a deep breath. "I know who killed Mikhail. A policeman stabbed him over and over." Rachel hung her head and wept. "Mikhail called him 'Uncle' and cried out for help. But the man kept stabbing him. And another man, who was fat and silent, just stood beside Mikhail and did nothing."

Nucia gasped. "Oh…tell me you're lying. Please, tell me it's not true."

"I wish I was lying. I wish I had never seen it," cried Rachel. "I can't tell the police because a policeman was the killer."

Nucia sat on the bench, moaning into her hands. "What you've seen is…is horrible." She reached out and hugged Rachel to her. "You must never tell anyone what you saw, Rachel." Nucia pulled back and grasped Rachel's shoulders. "Our whole family could be in danger if you tell anybody, especially Father…he will insist on going to the police. Promise?"

Rachel choked back her tears. "I promise." Though she'd worried about confiding in her sister, Rachel felt lighter somehow, relieved of her heavy load.

❄❄❄

Sergei frowned at the clock hanging on the wall at the front of the classroom. Another hour of lessons. He knew he should be working on his arithmetic problems, but he couldn't focus. Sergei turned his paper over and began drawing a picture of his teacher, Mr. Bogdanov, sitting at the front of the class, his eyes partially concealed beneath bushy red eyebrows.

Sergei peered at Mr. Bogdanov and drew his face with cross-hatching to denote his ruddy complexion. As he drew, Sergei couldn't stop thinking about Mikhail. He used to love Sergei's drawings and had encouraged him to become an artist. Mikhail had dreamed of studying at the university in Petersburg. Together they'd talked excitedly about their future, away from Kishinev and their families' expectations that hindered their dreams.

He examined his caricature of Bogdanov and was pleased with what he saw. He'd captured the teacher's swarthy eyes, and the gigantic nose was an excellent parody of the real thing. He looked up and saw Mr. Bogdanov glaring at him.

"Sergei, do you have a question?" asked Mr. Bogdanov.

"No, sir."

Bring your work up to me so I can see it for myself."

Sergei walked slowly to the front of the room. He lay the paper down in front of Mr. Bogdanov and stared at his feet.

"Umm. I see that arithmetic is not on your agenda today. Have you become an expert at mathematics overnight?"

"No, sir."

"Do you feel that rubbish such as this is a better use of your time than the arithmetic I teach?"

"No, sir."

"Then why are you wasting my time and the class's time?" Mr. Bogdanov crushed Sergei's drawing in his hands and threw it in the bin.

"I don't know." Sergei hung his head.

"Well, since you can't be trusted to do your work on your own, you will now sit up at the front with me so I can keep an eye on you. And I will inform your parents of your insolence."

Sergei bit his lips and clenched his fists. His father was going to be furious when he found out that Sergei had been disrespectful. As he dropped into the chair beside his teacher, Sergei started to devise a plan to get away from Kishinev.

❄❄❄

"We can't wait any longer to eat," said Sergei's mother. "I don't know where your father is. More than likely police business has kept him. Come, Sergei, Natalya. Come Carlotta. Make haste to the table."

"Mama, how many more days of Lent are there?" asked Natalya when they sat down to their dinner of halibut and boiled potatoes.

"It hasn't even been a week, child," answered her mother. "There are still six weeks to go."

"Oh," groaned Natalya. "I miss eating eggs and meat and sweets. And I am so tired of fish."

Carlotta piled her plate with halibut and passed the fish to Sergei. "Any fish is good if it is on a hook."

Sergei raised his brow and smiled at Natalya, who had both hands over her mouth, giggling over Carlotta's words.

"Sergei, put more on your plate. Eat. Come now. Eat," his mother said when he took only one small piece.

"I'm not very hungry, Mama."

"Are you in love?" Natalya asked him.

"Natalya!" said Sergei's mother.

"Maria says that when people fall in love they can't eat or sleep. How do they stay alive without food or sleep? Is that what happened to you, Mama?"

Carlotta belched and put her hand to her mouth. Both Sergei and Natalya snickered at their aunt's table manners.

"Good heavens! The words that come out of your mouth Natalya," said Sergei's mother, ignoring Carlotta. "It's a good thing your father's not here. Now, enough of your chatter. Eat. Both of you."

Sergei's father sauntered in just as they finished, bringing a waft of cold air, tobacco, and alcohol into the room. "What the devil...have I missed supper? I was tied up with the second autopsy of that Rybachenko boy." He stomped his feet, hung up his coat, and crossed himself. "Another idiot concluded there was no sign of a blood sacrifice. But I don't believe this man any more than the Jew who did the first examination." He turned to face Sergei directly. "I ran into Mr. Bogdanov at the tavern. He told me you've been wasting your time drawing pictures instead of doing the required lesson."

"The tavern? But it's Lent, Aleksandr," said Sergei's mother.

Sergei slumped in his chair, knowing what was about to come. His father waved his mother away and stood on the other side of the table, glaring at Sergei.

"It was a review class, and I was tired of doing the same problems over and over," said Sergei.

"You were tired," said his father in a mocking tone. "So you decided to do what you wanted rather than what you were told to do."

"I'm sorry."

"And why the silly pictures?" asked his father. He poured himself a large glass of vodka, held his head back, and took a big drink.

"They're not silly. I like to draw. It's not a crime, is it?" Sergei wanted to yell out that he wanted to become an artist, but his father was already full of vodka and rage. Sergei finished his dinner and went to bed, feeling as worthless as the crumpled piece of paper his teacher had thrown away.

MARCH

As Easter approaches, we need to come together, fellow Christians, to purge our town of Jews.

—Bessarabetz, *March 29, 1903*

One

Rachel wrapped herself in her threadbare coat and walked out to the courtyard past the Berlatsky children getting ready for a snowball fight. Though it was late in the afternoon, the air was still warm, hinting of spring.

"Rachel!" Chaia's little brother, Jacob, waved at her, his curly blond hair hanging in his face.

Rachel waved back and saw they'd divided themselves into teams. Jacob and Chaia were behind a shed, and had only a few snowballs compared to their older sisters, Elena and Esther, who had a pyramid of them stacked next to the ice cellar.

"Come play with us, Rachel," Chaia shouted.

Rachel was relieved that she had a reason to say no. She couldn't imagine taking part in a silly snowball fight when Mikhail's murder still haunted her day and night. "I was supposed to buy some thread on the way home from school today," she said in the most apologetic tone she could muster, "but I forgot. Mother will be angry if I don't have it."

Chaia laughed. "You're the most forgetful person I know!"

Rachel tightened the belt around her coat and walked briskly out of the courtyard.

"Wait, Rachel!" cried Chaia. "We're not supposed to leave the courtyard alone—"

"I'll be fine," Rachel called over her shoulder. She wanted to be by herself; since Mikhail's murder, she had not been alone for a single moment.

Rachel came out of the courtyard onto Stavrisky Street, the winding dirt road that led to upper Kishinev. Narrow branches wrapped with fresh snow were like larks' claws perched above the road. The street seemed much quieter than usual; only a small group of boys smoking and laughing on the sidewalk, and a couple of women strolling toward a house in the distance.

As she approached the market, Rachel stopped and glanced around, suddenly feeling guilty for not heeding her father's warning to stay in lower Kishinev. But she'd been coming to this market all of her life without a problem. Surely no harm could come from going directly to the shop. Feeling bold and somewhat courageous, Rachel marched forward, immediately passing pigs, quails, grouse, partridges chickens, and sheep standing on frozen legs, all covered in frost, all waiting patiently to be sold. Next to them rose neat piles of milk in icy brick shapes.

"It boils! It boils! Will nobody drink?"

An elderly tea seller was trying to make a few more sales before the end of the day. Around his waist was a leather case filled with glasses; a bag of cakes and lemons was slung over his shoulder. The steam from his samovar rose in delicate swirls and then disappeared into the air. A few peddlers stood warming their hands over a nearby bonfire.

Makovsky's was a gray brick store with a red door and window frame, squeezed between a tavern and a restaurant. Inside, one entire wall was devoted to threads and wool, arranged by color from lightest to darkest, so that it looked like a brilliant rainbow. This large selection was the reason Rachel's mother preferred this shop to the Jewish one near their house. Rachel looked around in silent delight. She didn't like to use a needle and thread, but the wonderful colors brightened her mood.

"Hurry up, child. Make up your mind." The shopkeeper glared at her over the counter. He began to complain loudly to the other person in the store, a well-dressed woman with a fancy embroidered headpiece and an overcoat trimmed in fur.

"They're all the same, abominations and parasites, like it says in the newspaper," he grumbled. "They come in here, take their time looking, and then buy one or two of my cheapest items, even though they have more money than the rest of us. And it's worse since they killed that poor boy." He leaned forward. "Why, I read that his eyes, ears, and mouth were sewn shut. And he had no blood left in his body." He handed the woman's purchases to her in a basket.

"Are you sure?" asked the woman. "I heard there were stab marks on him, but nothing about his eyes or ears."

"I know what I read. And now the Jews feel guilty about one of their own committing such a vicious crime, so fewer of them are showing their faces," said the shopkeeper, spitting out the sharp words like poison darts.

Rachel listened in disbelief. The shopkeeper was speaking

as if Rachel could not hear his venomous words. She had done nothing, said nothing to provoke this man, yet he despised her as if she were guilty of a crime. She backed up while the shopkeeper leered at her like a snake eyeing its prey. The woman eyed her with pity but said nothing.

"Get on with you," he shouted at Rachel. "As if you were going to spend money in here anyway. Get out of here, you Jewish pest!"

Rachel walked out of the store, her head held high, tears streaming down her face. As she hurried along the crowded sidewalks, faces blurred and her breathing accelerated. She knew that her black coat and shawl reflected her Jewish faith, her respect for tradition, and she wore them proudly, like a badge of honor. But after the shopkeeper's hateful words, she felt like one of the animals on display in the market, to be sold and devoured. She stepped up her pace in order to get home before anyone saw the tears in her eyes.

Forging straight ahead, she didn't see the group of girls lurking in the doorway of a boarded-up store until they were almost upon her. As Rachel walked past, they grabbed hold of her arm and kicked her in the shins.

"Stop...please, stop!" cried Rachel. Her legs were burning, but the girls now had a firm grip on her waist and shoulders. She couldn't get away or fight back.

"Stupid Yid!" The largest, strongest girl smacked Rachel across the top of her head.

"Let me go...leave me—" A punch in the gut took Rachel's breath away. She lurched forward.

"What do you think you're doing? Get away from here," demanded a familiar, husky voice.

A pair of strong hands broke Rachel's fall. She turned her head to see who had saved her and was astounded to see Sergei.

❄❄❄

Sergei had been on his way home for dinner when he heard a girl scream for help. To his surprise, he saw Rachel, being battered and falling forward. He caught her, stopping her from collapsing onto her face.

"Get away from here," he yelled at the girls.

"Stupid Yid," snarled one of them. She spat at Rachel and moved down the street, the rest of the girls following like a herd of sheep.

"Th…thank you," Rachel whispered, straightening her body slowly. "I think…I'll be all right now."

"Are you sure?" Sergei could already see a nasty bump developing on her forehead.

She nodded, smoothed her hair, and wiped her face. Sergei was impressed by her courage, her ability to stand tall and pretend nothing had happened. Remembering the Jews he'd seen harassed in the square, he shuddered. Like Rachel, they'd done nothing to provoke their attackers. He wanted Rachel to know that he was different from these girls, a better person.

"I've…" He swallowed and started again. "I've been meaning to tell you that I'm sorry about…when I knocked the flour out of your arms. It was an accident, and I should have stopped to help you."

Rachel's jaw dropped. "Why didn't you?"

He took a deep breath and considered his answer. There was no way he could admit to Rachel that he became nervous in her presence, but he couldn't lie to her either. He decided to avoid the question entirely. "I wanted to, but…let me make it up to you. I'll walk you home, to make sure you get there safely."

The corners of Rachel's lips turned up slightly, making Sergei's heart skip a beat. "I feel terrible about the way those girls treated you," he said as they headed south, to lower Kishinev. The sun was going down, tinting the sky a grayish-lavender, and a streetcar rumbled past.

"It's not your fault," Rachel replied slowly, her head down. "Ever since Mikhail…people, like those girls, act as if we're all guilty."

Sergei stuck his hands in his pockets and felt her shawl. He turned around and walked backwards, facing Rachel, ignoring the rest of the people rushing past. "Can I ask you something?"

She stopped and lifted her head. "I guess so…"

"Why do people say that Jews killed Mikhail for his blood?"

Rachel sighed. "That's just a stupid rumor. It's been around forever."

Sergei locked her in his gaze, waiting for her to continue.

"When *matzah* is a few days old, or gets wet, a red mold appears."

"And matzah is…?"

"A bread we make without flour for Passover, when we can't eat anything with wheat."

"So that's it?" Sergei turned and resumed walking with Rachel. "Just because this bread turns red, people think it's made with blood?"

"Yes, but it's against our religion to eat anything with blood." Rachel smiled wanly. "Silly, isn't it?"

"Ridiculous. And Mikhail would be so angry if he knew such lies were being spread about his murder. Even the newspaper is running stories about Jews crucifying him for his blood."

Rachel nodded. "I know. I want to be a writer, a journalist perhaps, but now—I don't trust newspapers anymore."

Sergei stopped and faced Rachel. "You shouldn't give up on becoming a writer because of a few crooked journalists. I'm sure there are many honest writers working at good newspapers."

"You don't think I'm crazy for wanting to write, even though I'm a girl?"

He shook his head and started walking again. "My sister is smart, like you. I want her to be able to do what she wants, not get stuck cooking and cleaning for a drunken husband." Sergei blushed, hearing the words that came out of his mouth. He hoped Rachel didn't realize he was talking about his father.

"You have a sister?"

"Natalya. She's eight," said Sergei, relieved Rachel showed interest in his sister only.

"She's lucky to have a big brother looking out for her." Rachel stopped and glanced at the walled courtyard behind them.

Sergei realized they were standing in the shabbiest part of town. There were no sidewalks, just a muddy pathway alongside the street. The courtyard walls were gray cement, cracked with age. Through the narrow opening into the courtyard, Sergei caught a glimpse of tiny, sagging houses with low, tiled roofs. They looked tired and worn out, the way Rachel appeared now, standing before him with dishevelled hair, holes in her stockings, and blood on her face. Still, her deep-set green eyes, and high cheekbones overshadowed her injuries. He imagined himself painting her face. He was intrigued by the mystery of Rachel and her culture that was as foreign to him as America. She wasn't like the other girls he knew, silly and giggling all the time about nothing of importance. Rachel was more thoughtful, more interesting, and much prettier.

"Thank you for walking me home," she said. "And for coming to my rescue."

"Any time." He paused. "But you should be more careful, until all of the anger and lies are gone."

"That's what my father told me."

"He sounds like a smart person."

"He is, very smart."

Sergei smiled. "Maybe we can talk again?"

She raised her eyes to meet his. "I'd like that."

He watched Rachel disappear inside the courtyard and then shuffled home slowly, fingering her shawl, which was still in his pocket. Sergei knew he should have returned it, but he liked having something that reminded him of Rachel, and it gave him a reason to see her again.

Two

Sergei tugged at the stiff red collar around his neck. He and his family were part of a growing procession of people on their way to Mass. The Orthodox cathedral's church bells rang out, occasionally muffled by the clip-clop of horses drawing carriages full of people.

"I hate wearing these clothes to church," Sergei complained to his mother. "I don't think *anybody* cares what we look like when we pray."

"You should be grateful you have such nice things to wear," his mother replied. "Especially at such an important time as Lent."

"I love dressing up," said Natalya, grinning at Sergei.

Just before they reached the impressive stone and iron gates leading to the cathedral, they saw men and women in ragged clothes begging for money to buy food. Sergei looked away when he smelled their poverty,fixing his eyes on the three-tiered belfry with its domed roof.

"Please sir, a few coins for our convent?" A gaunt woman in a long black robe held out her hand. Her skin was so white that her eyebrows looked like sticks on snow. Sergei's father reached into his front pocket, pulled out a few kopecks, and handed them to her.

As he watched, Sergei wished that his father could be generous and kind every day, not just on Sundays.

Entering the pale yellow cathedral, Sergei approached the icons and kissed them, a custom that was entrenched in his Sunday routine. As the crowd filled the cathedral, Sergei was pressed so tightly against other people that he could smell their skin, their smelly sheepskin coats, and their stale breath. Yet when the procession entered, the throng of people divided. The soft murmur of voices stopped instantly when the priest walked through the Royal Door at the back of the building, dressed in full ecclesiastical vestments. The fragrant incense and smoldering odor of burning candles filled the church, creating a soft haze in the air.

"Let us pray," said the priest in a commanding tone.

After an hour of standing, singing, chanting, and crossing himself, Sergei was ready to go home. He looked down at Natalya, whose head was at people's waists. She was drooping from the heat and the crowd. Sergei squeezed her warm, sticky hand. She gave him a look of desperation.

"Can we go now?" he asked his mother, wedged in beside him.

"Shh..." she whispered. "The choir is about to sing."

Sergei listened. The men's voices, unaccompanied by instruments, sounded simple and pure. People standing near

Sergei closed their eyes as the voices soared. He wondered if any of these men and women were responsible for spreading the rumors about Mikhail's body being sewn shut. But it was impossible to see beyond people's skin and into their hearts and minds.

When the service ended, Sergei, still holding Natalya's hand, worked his way through the congregation with his parents. Outside, he saw Mikhail's grandparents for the first time since the funeral. Looking old and stooped, they walked alone, carefully descending the steps of the church. Sergei remembered how Mikhail used to place his arm around his grandmother when they left the cathedral, so that she appeared upright and proud. Now she looked fragile and defeated.

"Sergei, we must greet Mikhail's grandparents," said his mother. "Natalya, you stay here with Papa."

"I don't know what to say," Sergei protested.

"Come." His mother firmly nudged him toward Mikhail's grandparents. "Good afternoon," she said effusively.

Sergei's voice was dry with apprehension. "Hello."

His mother continued. "It is so nice to see you. How are you coping? Is there anything we can do for you?" She touched Mikhail's grandmother lightly on the shoulder.

"We're as well as can be expected," said Mikhail's grandfather. He had the same sharp blue eyes as Mikhail, and brown spots on his pale, almost translucent, face.

Mikhail's grandmother looked up and smiled wearily. She had white hair and waxy looking skin. Over her black overcoat hung Mikhail's silver cross, the one he'd worn since his birth. When he saw it, Sergei's throat constricted. Somehow, seeing Mikhail's icon on his grandmother made everything that had happened so real and final.

Mikhail's grandfather gazed at Sergei solemnly. "Excuse us, we must go."

"Of course," said Sergei's mother. "I will pray for you."

Mikhail's grandmother's eyes filled with tears. She took her husband's arm and started to walk away. As she did, she turned around and stared at Sergei. All he could see was Mikhail's silver icon sparkling brightly against her coat.

❄❄❄

Sergei sat hunched on the bench watching his friends skate. This was the first time he'd been back to the river since he'd come with his father, when blood had stained the ice. Now he felt guilty for being here, as if he was betraying his friend by being alive.

Petya skated in front of the bench. "Come on, Sergei. The ice is going to break in a couple of weeks."

Grimacing, Sergei stood up, stepped onto the ice, and followed Petya to their group of friends skating toward the bend in the river. When he passed the spot where he last saw Mikhail, he held his breath.

"Sergei's here," announced Petya, stopping suddenly on the ice and nodding toward him.

"Good. Let's race to where the river narrows," said Theodore. "On the count of three...one, two, three!"

The boys were off in a flurry, commanding the ice as they flew by parents teaching small children to skate, young people practicing turns, and older couples gliding sedately along the frozen river.

Sergei started slowly, swinging his arms from side to side.

All he could think about was how Mikhail would never be able to skate again, or do any of the other things he had loved to do. Eventually, the cold air cleared his head, making him feel a little bit better. He picked up speed, but Nikolai, tall and lean, had already arrived, followed by Theodore and Petya.

"Hey, let's sit over there." Nikolai skated to the river's edge where an immense tree trunk had fallen on its side years ago. He pulled himself up to sit on it and gestured to the others to join him.

"I can't stay for long," said Sergei. "My father gets mad if I'm out too late."

"What does The Beard do? Interrogate you?" asked Theodore, with a sly grin. "Isn't he busy looking for Mikhail's killer?"

Nikolai undid his skate blades, stood up, and walked gingerly along a thick branch overhanging the river. His hair was shaved so close to his scalp that his head reflected the afternoon sun. "My father says it's only a matter of time before the guilty Jew is caught."

"How does your father know it's a Jew?" asked Petya.

"Petya's right. It may not be a Jew. Those stories about Jews killing for blood aren't true." Sergei watched as Nikolai swayed and almost fell off the branch, then managed to regain his balance. "Why don't you get off that branch?"

"Who are you? My mother?" Sneering, Nikolai stood on one leg and teetered back and forth, then walked back along the branch toward the boys.

"How do you know those stories aren't true?" Theodore asked, frowning at Sergei. "I've seen the headlines in the newspaper about Jews needing blood to make bread."

Sergei scowled at Theodore. "Don't believe everything you read."

"Did you hear that another Russian—a girl—was killed yesterday?" asked Nikolai, as he picked at the dry bark of the tree with his bare hands.

"What are you talking about?" said Sergei.

"Some girl who worked as a housemaid for a Jewish doctor. There were wounds on her heels and people say she was killed for her blood, like Mikhail."

"That's crazy. What people? And how do you know they weren't making the whole story up?" asked Sergei.

Nikolai stood up and kicked at the bark. "My mother heard people talking about the girl at the market." He jumped down from the branch. "Why would people make up a story like that?"

"Because—" Sergei took a deep breath. "Rachel told me that their bread turns red when it gets wet or is old, from mold. That's why people think it's made with blood."

"When were you talking to Rachel?" asked Theodore.

"A few days ago."

"And you believe what *she* says?" said Nikolai.

"Mikhail would have believed her," said Petya. "Why shouldn't Sergei?"

"So now you two are Jew lovers, like Mikhail," scoffed Theodore. "Look where that got him."

"We're not Jew lovers," argued Petya. "But can you honestly believe that Jews would kill people and make food from their blood? It just seems so…so…"

"Idiotic," said Sergei.

Petya slipped off the tree trunk and began attaching his skate blades to his boots. "We all believe Jesus rose from the dead, which might seem stupid to them." He stood and started skating back.

Sergei, Nikolai, and Theodore jumped onto the ground, attached their skate blades, and followed Petya.

"My father says the Jews are going to have a surprise soon. Maybe at Easter," said Nikolai, rushing to the lead and turning around to skate backwards, facing the others.

"How can he be sure?" asked Sergei.

Nikolai shrugged his shoulders. "He says we need to get rid of a lot of the Jews, that there are more than fifty thousand here in Kishinev now, half of our entire population." Nikolai turned around again so that he was facing the same direction as everyone else.

"I heard my father tell my uncle that the Jews have helped make Kishinev successful, because they run better businesses than Russians do," said Petya.

"That's why my father lost his job," said Theodore with obvious reproach. "The flour mill he worked for closed down because it couldn't compete with the Jewish mill."

"But there's nothing illegal about running a good business," argued Sergei.

Petya nodded. "You can't force Jews to leave just because they're successful."

"They're lashing out at us," said Theodore. "Look at Mikhail and now this Russian girl. We have to do something to show them we're not going to sit here and let them destroy us."

"What does your father say, Sergei?" asked Petya.

"Well, he can't do anything without proof. He's been interviewing people—"

"But what does he think?" asked Nikolai.

The three boys stopped skating and looked at Sergei expectantly.

"He thinks a Jew killed Mikhail, but he has no evidence, in fact the medical examiner—"

"You see, even The Beard knows the truth. He doesn't need proof to know what happened," Theodore said.

Sergei swallowed and found his throat was scratchy and dry. "I don't want to talk about this anymore."

"Wait and see," warned Nikolai. "Something's going to happen soon."

Three

"Why don't you dress as Esther?" Rachel suggested to Nucia. The girls were standing by the bench they slept on, clothing scattered all over the floor.

"Half the girls from the shul will be Esther." Nucia held up a faded black skirt. "Look at this rag. You can see where the seams have been let out twice!"

Rachel held the skirt up and frowned. "Maybe you can wear something of Mother's."

"This *was* Mother's," replied Nucia. She grabbed the skirt from Rachel and threw it on the floor.

"Nucia, you'll look beautiful no matter what you wear."

Nucia scowled at Rachel and held her face in her hands.

"What's going on in here?" asked their mother. She stood with her hands on her hips surveying the mess.

"I can't find a costume to wear for Purim," said Nucia. "We don't have anything."

"Enough already." Rachel's mother shook her head. "Just choose something. And put this clothing away where it belongs."

"But I want to look different from everyone else," said Nucia.

"You should have so many dresses…a different one for every day! You should be so lucky…I should be so lucky." Rachel's mother went back behind the curtain, mumbling loudly about craziness.

"Ohh—" groaned Nucia. She threw herself face down, banging her fist on the bench.

Rachel finished buttoning her father's black shirt and put on his black cap which completed her Haman costume. Haman was the evil character in the story of Esther who tried to have all the Jews in Persia killed. But in the end, Haman was killed and the Jews survived. Every year, Rachel dressed as Haman for Purim because she liked pretending to be evil. Now, she pictured Haman as the policeman who had killed Mikhail.She blinked to get the disturbing image out of her head and thought of another idea for Nucia. "Why don't you be Vashti? You know, the first queen of Persia who refused to appear before the king's guests and was banished."

"There's no point in choosing costumes this year," interrupted their father in a flat voice as he walked into the house.

"What do you mean?" asked Rachel. She and Nucia pushed the curtain aside and joined their parents.

Her father cleared his throat and sat down on the bench by the stove. "Rabbi Yitzchak has decided that costumes are not appropriate this year, given the somber mood in Kishinev right now."

"But you can't have Purim without costumes," said Nucia.

Rachel gazed down at her Haman costume. "What do our costumes have to do with the rest of Kishinev? I don't understand..."

Her father shook his head.

"Come, Rachel, get out of those clothes," said her mother. "And Nucia help clean up this mess."

❄❄❄

"Father, it won't seem like Purim with so many people missing," Rachel whispered when she saw the meager turnout at shul. Rabbi Yitzchak began the service with a special prayer and then carefully took the scroll containing the Book of Esther from the sacred Ark. Flanked by twisted columns, the Ark was in the middle of the synagogue on a raised platform.

When the story of Esther was finished, Rachel began fidgeting in her seat. Her mind drifted to the River Byk; she saw it meander on the north side of Kishinev, frozen and white. Then she spotted a crack right down the middle, dividing the river in half. Rachel closed her eyes and the image of the river grew and grew until she could see the jagged edges of the crack break apart. Blood seeped through the ice and spread across the river until it was an angry red. Rachel jumped, her eyes wide open. Perspiration beaded down her forehead and her hands shook. She turned to her mother, whose gaze was fixed on the Ark below.

"Traditionally, our Purim celebration would begin now," the rabbi said cautiously. "But—" he sighed. "I've decided, in light of the current situation, that such boisterous activities are not suitable this year."

Rachel saw her mother's mouth set in a hard line. Nucia gave Rachel an incredulous look and turned back to the rabbi.

"Today," Rabbi Yitzchak continued in a grave voice, "we are facing a real Haman in Kishinev—Pavolachi Krushevan, editor of the gentile newspaper, the *Bessarabetz*. His scandalous stories bear no semblance to the truth. He wants to rid Kishinev of Jews, even though we have lived in relative harmony here for twenty-four years."

"This is all because people think Jews killed Mikhail. We need to tell the truth about what happened," Rachel whispered to Nucia.

Nucia shook her head and looked back at the rabbi.

"Fear has taken hold of our community," he said. "The fear of walking alone, the fear of strangers, and the fear of attending shul. We must remain strong and united, and purge our enemies of their hatred and lust for violence. Only then will we have our freedom, without fear."

Rachel agonized over the rabbi's words. One newspaper editor was affecting the lives of all the Jews here today. It was hard to believe that one man's printed words held such power. Maybe Sergei was right, she thought. Maybe she should try even harder to become a writer, an honest writer, so that the truth could be told one day.

❄❄❄

"Would you like my pastry?" asked Sacha. He sat across from Rachel at her family's table, which was laden with food. "There are no more left and I already had one."

Rachel looked down at the *hamantashen* with its sweet

seed filling and felt a wave of nausea. She was so full it hurt. She hadn't eaten this much food in months. In the Purim tradition, neighbors, friends and even strangers, wealthy Jews from north Kishinev, had delivered food to their doorstep that morning. All of it was so good, the potatoes fried with butter and onions, the thick cabbage soup, the black bread layered with extra butter, and the hamantashen—the triangular-shaped pastry that represented Haman's hat.

"No, thank you. I'm full," she replied, glancing up and meeting Sacha's eyes. He'd been staring at her all evening, which made her nervous. She fiddled with her hair and licked her lips, worried that she had food on her face.

Sasha shrugged and ate the hamantashen in two bites. "Your father told me about those girls and what they did to you. Are you feeling all right? You look a little pale."

"Yes. I'm fine," said Rachel, managing a weak smile. She twirled her braid with her fingers.

"Do you want to go for a walk? The fresh air might be good for you."

For some reason, Rachel was suddenly uncomfortable with Sacha. He was paying too much attention to her, and being far too kind. Rachel had never considered Sacha as anything other than a friend, almost family, for they had spent so many holiday dinners together. He was like a brother to her. She could never imagine him as anything else.

"I don't think so," she said with a rueful smile. "I'm very tired today."

Disappointment flickered across Sacha's face. Rachel felt bad for causing him pain, but thought it was better he knew now that she didn't return his feelings, rather than later. She turned to her father who was speaking with Sacha's father.

"How about some more wine, Gofsha?" asked Mr. Talansky.

"Gladly," said her father. He stood up to pour some dark red wine into Mr. Talansky's clay cup.

"Did you ever meet with Bishop Iakov?" Mr. Talansky continued.

Rachel's father took a sip of his wine. "Yes. We hoped he would spread the word that the tale about Mikhail being killed for blood was nothing more than a myth." He cleared his throat, put his cup on the table, and reached into the pouch he carried around his waist for a cigarette. "The bishop was evasive, unwilling to promise anything, and even said it was useless to deny that Jews use Christian blood for ritual purposes." He shook his head and lit the cigarette.

"I guess we can't expect much help from the Orthodox Church then," said Mr. Talansky.

Rachel's mother and Nucia started to clear the dishes off the table. Rachel stood and prepared to help. "If we can't convince a bishop, then how will we ever convince anybody that these rumors are crazy?" she asked.

"With great difficulty. It's almost like we're speaking a different language, yet we live and work alongside these people," said Mr. Talansky. "The problem is that there are so many falsehoods and stories circulating. As soon as one ends another begins."

"Why doesn't somebody write an article for the newspaper that explains how these rumors started?" asked Sacha.

"Because the gentiles can't read our Yiddish paper and they would never have an article written by a Jew in theirs," said Rachel's father.

Mr. Talansky grunted, a deep throaty sound that startled Rachel. "Well, we need to find some way to convince gentiles that we're not savage animals. Before Passover, so that everyone feels safe to attend shul." He held out his empty cup to Rachel's father for more wine.

"The best thing would be if Mikhail's *real* killer is found." Rachel piled some plates in the enamel washbasin and stared at Nucia with pleading eyes.

"I'm sure the *police* are doing all they can," said Nucia firmly.

Rachel touched the amber necklace around her neck and wondered if she had made a wise decision in revealing her secret to Nucia and then promising to keep it forever. Sometimes she felt the burden was more than she could bear.

❄❄❄

I have ruined Purim for all the Jews in Kishinev, she wrote in her journal that evening. *Even the rabbi is afraid to honor our traditions because of the bad feelings toward us. I want to go to Mikhail's grandparents and tell them how sorry I am. They deserve to know how their grandson died, yet I cannot say a word.*

If I had not forgotten my shawl that day, then I wouldn't have Mikhail's murder embalmed in my brain. I would not have to bear this secret like a scar.

❄❄❄

Sergei and his father were on their way to the bathhouse when they ran into Zinaida Ustyug, a scrawny little man who lived in their building. Sergei cringed when his father stopped to talk to him. He had a hoarse, guttural voice, and when he spoke, an oversized lump moved up and down his neck.

"Might be some trouble ahead," said Zinaida to Sergei's father.

"What kind of trouble, hmm?" Sergei's father scratched his head and looked at man.

"Some—" Zinaida broke into a coughing fit that lasted several minutes. "Some Moldavian farmers," he continued. "I saw them at the tavern a couple of days ago. They were telling anybody who'd listen how they need to fight to protect themselves from the Jews."

Sergei shook his head in disbelief and looked at his father.

"And just what were these farmers proposing to do?"

"Beat the Jews. That's what they said. During the Easter holidays. I thought you should know."

"Have you seen these men since?"

"I saw them walking around the main square yesterday, handing out leaflets, but I didn't have time to get one for myself. I had to get back to the factory."

"Very well. I'll look into it." Sergei's father nodded at Zinaida and continued to the bathhouse.

"What are you going to do about those Moldavians Zinaida mentioned?" asked Sergei as they removed their clothes in the change area, a small square room with a wooden bench that ran around the perimeter. A couple of other men were getting ready for their baths as well.

"Nothing. Those men were just talking. Zinaida didn't even see the leaflet. Everything will pass."

"But what if Zinaida is right? What if a big fight—"

Sergei's father grabbed his son's arm tightly, squeezing until his skin burned. "I told you to stop interfering and I mean it." He released Sergei's arm and pulled open the heavy door leading to the steam room.

Sergei clenched his jaw and reluctantly followed his father into the hot-steam area, with its large glass windows, smooth linden-wood benches, and high ceiling. The room smelled of burnt wood and sweat. Sergei lay face down on a bench and let the boiling hot mist envelop his body, releasing sweat and dirt. After a few minutes, the bathhouse worker began beating Sergei's back vigorously with soapy birch brooms.

As his body was joggled over and over, Sergei wished he could be a bathhouse worker for a few minutes and strike his father's back. He would hit him so hard, he wouldn't be able to get up.

Just when he could stand it no more, the beating stopped, and Sergei sat up. His pewter icon burned his chest, reminding him of the Sabbath the next day. On the bench across from him, his father was receiving the cupping treatment. The masseur ignited cotton and inserted heat into glass cups, which were then stuck to his father's back. This treatment was supposed to cure nagging back problems.

Sergei headed to the other end of the large room where there was a cold-water shower. He turned the knob and gritted his teeth as the cold water collided with his hot skin producing a stinging sensation. When his body temperature cooled, the burning subsided. After a couple of minutes, Sergei left the shower and returned to the heat.

"Any progress on that boy's murder, Aleksandr?" said Mr. Ulrich, who was lying across from Sergei's father, his withered skin sagging from protruding bones.

Sergei scowled. Although he wanted nothing more than to find Mikhail's killer, he was tired of listening to people prying his father for information.

"Not yet," said Sergei's father.

"I think Jews killed that Rybachenko boy and that housemaid. For blood. Like it says in the papers."

Sergei glowered at Mr. Ulrich, disgusted by idiots like him who believed in such rubbish without any proof.

"I'm not sure anymore," disagreed Dmitry Chesnokov, a young man who was being cupped as he spoke. "There was an article in the newspaper this morning that said the previous stories about the boy's murder were not based on any proof. An autopsy found that he died from stab wounds, not some ritual killing."

"That's a cover-up because Jews have pressured the editors to stop the rumors," Mr. Ulrich argued. "The Jews are getting scared about what people will do to them if their secret, barbaric rituals are exposed."

"I agree," said Sergei's father. He sat up on his bench with his hands on his thick, hairy knees. "The sooner the Jews are exposed as animals, the better."

Sergei clenched his fists.

"So you still think the murderer was a Jew?" asked Dmitry.

"Probably—"

"But you don't know for sure, Papa," Sergei argued. "You don't have any information about Mikhail's killer." He flinched under his father's withering glare, knowing he should have kept his mouth shut. But he wanted to defend the Jews, for Rachel and the other innocent people he had seen being attacked.

"How dare you contradict me," his father hissed under his breath. "Get out of here right now."

Sergei stomped out of the steam area, pulled his clothes over his perspiring body, and left. All he could think about was Rachel, and how she and the rest of the Jews in Kishinev had no chance against people like his father who drew horrible conclusions without any proof.

❄❄❄

"I can't wait to eat lots of cakes, anything sweet," said Petya to Nikolai and Sergei. They were walking on the slushy sidewalks with a large crowd of boys from their school to Chuflinskii Square where they often gathered. The street was littered with horse excrement and rubbish that had been hidden for months by the snow.

"Me too, but there's still another week and a half to go until Easter and the end of Lent," said Nikolai. His voice cracked as he spoke. It was changing from a high-pitched boy's voice to a young man's.

Sergei stomped his feet as he walked, splashing the slush onto his leather boots. "I want to eat meat again and drink milk."

Nikolai pointed ahead. "Look, Jews in the square."

Sergei's heart sank when he saw a Jewish woman and two children walking through the middle of the square. The woman looked up with fear in her eyes when she heard the boys talking and laughing. Sergei figured there were at least twenty boys now focused on the woman and children, two girls who appeared to be around six and eight years old.

"Let's go to the tobacco shop," said Sergei loudly, to distract everyone from the Jews.

"Later," said Nikolai. He and some other boys were already moving swiftly toward the woman and girls.

"Come on. Now." Sergei panicked when he remembered what a small number of girls had done to Rachel. With a crowd of boys, these people could be badly hurt. He looked around and saw eyes filled with rage directed at the Jews. Only he and Petya stood back as the rest of the boys advanced like a pack of wolves ready to attack a deer.

"Nikolai, Orest, Ivan, Dmitry…stop. Please," called Sergei to the boys leading the crowd. "They're not harming you…leave them alone."

"Quiet, Sergei," hissed Petya. "You're going to be next if you don't keep your mouth shut."

"But this is wrong. You know this is horrible. It's a woman and her children. They can't defend themselves."

"I know, but there's nothing we can do. And if you keep yelling at them to stop, they'll think you're betraying them and go after *you*."

"How can you just stand there and do *nothing*, Petya? You live beside Jews, you have a sister and a mother. Would you want them to be struck by a mob like this?"

Petya looked away.

"Don't hurt my children!" The woman's frightened voice rose above the loud, cheerful carousel music.

Sergei looked toward the carousel, watching the colorful carved horses revolving around the mirror, immune to the tension that was growing like a winter storm. He heard shouts and saw his friends kicking the woman and her children, throwing the vegetables and fruit she had purchased onto the ground. He looked frantically around the square for a policeman but saw nobody. "Damm! Come with me to stop them," he said to Petya. "I can't take them on by myself."

"I won't join our friends, but I can't turn on them either," said Petya. He started to drift away from the woman and children who lay groaning and crying on the muddy ground.

Sergei, repulsed by what he'd witnessed, disappointed by Petya, and disgusted by his inability to help, raced out of the square.

❄❄❄

Sergei heard his sister's voice chatting happily before he opened the door to their flat. She was perched on a chair at the table cutting leaves out of paper. His mother was stirring cabbage soup on the stove, and Carlotta was setting the table, humming as she worked. Though he was only a few blocks from the square, it felt like a completely different world.

"Papa..." Sergei strode toward his father who was adding some logs to the stove. "You have to send officers to the square. Some boys there are hurting a Jewish woman and her children."

His father stood up and wiped his hands.

"One of the girls is about Natalya's age."

"Why tell me? Why not tell an officer in the square?"

"There were no officers in sight."

Sergei's father sighed. "I will put extra men in the square tomorrow. It's too late to do anything now." He poured himself a glass of brandy and sat down on the sofa.

"Too late, but—"

"That's enough," growled his father. "I don't want to hear any more about this."

Sergei stared at him, unable and unwilling to believe he could be so casual about the safety of the woman and her children. "But Papa—"

"Sergei," said his mother. "Please don't get into an argument with Papa right now. He's had a very long day."

Sergei looked at his mother. Even she didn't care or didn't understand that a mother, like her, and her children were in danger.

"Look, Sergei!" Natalya held out a branch covered with handmade leaves and flowers. "Papa brought home this big pussy willow branch and I'm adding my own pretty leaves. Do you like it?"

It was the Fast Fair. Sergei had forgotten all about it. On the Thursday before Palm Sunday—today—children celebrated by carrying branches around the streets. He had no intention of taking part this year, especially after seeing his friends attacking innocent Jews in the square.

"It's very good," he said, giving his sister a distracted smile.

"You're going to come with me and carry a branch." Natalya held out a long pussy willow branch. "See, Papa brought you one as well."

"I think I'm too old for this now."

"But you have to come," cried Natalya, clutching Sergei's branch.

His mother stopped stirring and wiped her hands on her apron. "Good heavens. You must come. You've always loved marching around with a branch."

Sergei shook his head and looked from his mother to his

father. "I'm not a little child anymore. I'm going to be fifteen soon. Nobody else my age will be walking around with branches tonight."

His father set his glass on the table and sneered at Sergei. "Did you ask your friends?"

"Most of my friends were too busy attacking a Jewish mother and her children today," he replied. "I doubt any of them are going."

"Well, if nobody you know is there, then you don't have to worry about being seen, hmm? You're going to show that we are a happy, strong family. That's what Kishinev needs right now. To see families together." His father picked up his newspaper and turned away from Sergei.

"I'm not making leaves or anything," Sergei said, biting his lower lip.

"That's all right. I'll make them for you." Natalya resumed her leaf making with a broad smile across her little face.

❄❄❄

Sergei's branch was decorated with blue flowers and sparse green leaves, but he wished it was covered with real leaves so he could hide his face behind it. He dragged his feet as he joined hundreds of children marching noisily along streets. Hearing the excited, high-pitched voices around him, Sergei scowled. He looked behind to see if his father noticed how tall he was compared to the other children, but his father was busy waving and greeting people as he walked by. His mother, walking with Carlotta behind his father, looked happier than they'd been in ages, which slightly appeased his resentment at being forced to march along the streets of Kishinev with little children.

"Papa, can I have a gingerbread cross?" said Natalya, as they came upon a roadside booth that sold these.

Sergei's mouth watered at the thought of gingerbread. He followed his father and Natalya to the booth, which was swarming with people. The vendor, a fleshy man with a booming voice, was selling the crosses to the loudest bidders. Sergei cringed when his father barked out a command for five, his voice overtaking others who'd certainly been waiting much longer.

Sergei picked the largest gingerbread icon from his father's hand, and took a bite out of it. This was the only sweet thing he'd been allowed to eat since Lent began, yet it tasted dry and plain. He stared at the cross and became queasy. This icon was the most sacred symbol of their faith. It represented all that was good and noble. Yet the talk about blood and killing Jews went against everything the icon stood for. Just looking at his gingerbread cross, with a bit of the top missing, left a bitter taste in Sergei's mouth. When he was sure nobody was looking, he dropped it on the ground and smashed it with his boot.

Four

"Father says we can start attending shul again," Chaia reported to Rachel and Leah. The girls were walking home from school on late winter snow that was trampled and the color of strong tea. Rachel held up her long skirt to keep it from getting filthy, but the edges were already soggy.

"We'll be coming back to shul also," said Leah.

"Oh! That's wonderful! I've really missed you both," said Rachel. She let go of her skirt and watched as chunks of snow stuck to it. "But why now?"

"The newspaper," Chaia said. The girls stopped at a corner and waited while a carriage drove past. "My father said there was a long article about Mikhail's murder, and how there was never any proof that a Jewish person committed the crime."

"Really?" said Rachel. "My father never thought they'd write anything but negative words about us."

They continued across the street, dodging small piles of horse manure.

"I can't understand why people actually believed such nonsense in the first place," said Rachel. "Watch out!" She pulled Chaia out of the way of a man carrying a pyramid of cabbage on top of his head.

"Cabbage...cabbage...who will buy it?" he called out loudly.

"That would have been a disaster," said Chaia. She turned to continue home.

Leah said good-bye a couple of minutes later. She lived in a house closer to town than Chaia and Rachel.

"I'm so glad I don't have to spend another Shabbos stuck in my house with my brother and sisters," Chaia said to Rachel. "Shul will be almost a holiday!"

"My sister can be nasty, but your sisters and brother are the loudest people I've ever heard."

"Just think what it's like to live with them," said Chaia. "I'm never going to have children. And I'm going to marry a rich man who can buy me beautiful clothes and lots of food." She paused. "I don't think my mother has had a new dress in years, and I'm tired of wearing my sisters' old clothes. Oh look, Rachel!" Chaia stopped and pointed to a shop window. "Look at that beautiful bonnet!"

Rachel peered in the shop window at the extravagant bonnet made of gold silk and velvet, embroidered with pearls. "It looks really expensive," she said to Chaia.

"When I get married, I'm going to have a bonnet like that," said Chaia, her face pasted to the window. "If I must cover my hair in front of strangers, I should have the prettiest bonnet in all of Kishinev. Don't you agree, Rachel?"

"It is beautiful, yes. And you would look perfect in it with your golden hair." Rachel looked wistfully at Chaia's shiny blonde braids and wondered if Chaia and Yoram had spoken about marriage. Chaia spent a lot of time with Yoram but did not talk about him with Rachel anymore, not since Mikhail had died. Rachel liked to think Chaia didn't really care for Yoram, that Chaia would eventually come back to her as a close friend, but in her heart, Rachel knew she was probably mistaken.

The girls walked past a candle shop and a group of jesters and musicians who were creating a large crowd with their dancing and singing. One jester, dressed in royal blue, purple and red, grabbed Chaia's hand and tried to get her to dance with him. Chaia giggled and blushed, then pulled away. The jester gave her a sad face and moved on to another person. Chaia stayed close to Rachel until they were out of the area, and in front of a pastry shop.

"I wish I could buy as many cakes as I wanted," said Chaia, peering through the window. "I hate having to worry about how much things cost, or how to divide a small piece of meat six ways. That's why I'll only marry a wealthy man."

"I don't know if I'll get married," said Rachel, twisting her braid.

Chaia stopped walking and stared at Rachel. "Are you crazy? Every girl marries. What would you do if you didn't get married? How would you eat and buy nice things to wear?"

"Perhaps I would travel, see other countries, and then write about my experiences. Besides, who would want to marry me? I'm no good at needlework or sewing or cooking. The only thing I'm good at is reading, and that doesn't take care of a household."

"That's not true, Rachel. You're beautiful and fun…I know you miss Mikhail, but you could never have married him. There will be lots of other boys—nice Jewish boys like Yoram—who will want to marry you. You can't leave Kishinev! What would I do without you?"

"It's not like I'm going tomorrow," Rachel said as they entered their courtyard. "Maybe I'll never go. Maybe we'll grow old together here."

❄❄❄

Rachel was in checkmate. Her father had his black bishops headed for her white king on one side, and his rook was facing her king on the other side.

"There's nothing I can do." She ran her fingers back and forth over her forehead. "You win."

He scrutinized her and cleared his throat. "Your face has healed well, thank goodness."

"If Sergei hadn't come along, I'd be a real mess." Rachel shivered when she recalled those girls, so brutal and rough. "I wish I had listened to you and not gone to upper Kishinev by myself."

Her father shook his head and sighed. "You certainly paid a high price for being disobedient, my child. I'm just grateful Sergei was there to help you. He is a good person."

Rachel nodded and cast her gaze down at the chessboard. She couldn't stop thinking about Sergei, how he had intervened and protected her from those awful girls, and how attentively he had listened to her.

"I don't think your mind was on the game today," her father said. "You have to pay more attention next time."

"But you always beat me. I'll never be as good as you."

"Come now. I used to say the very same thing to my father, and then one day, I won. Just like that."

Rachel watched her father put the chess set carefully into its wooden box. He never let anyone else take it out or put it away. *Zeyde* had carved the wooden set for her father when he was a boy. "Why have we never met Zeyde? Whenever I ask about him and *Bubbe*, you tell me we will go to see them, but we never do. Do they live too far from here?"

Her father ran his hand over the box. "They live in Mohileff in the Gomel province, which is a good distance, but that's not why we haven't gone." He hesitated. "Zeyde and I had a disagreement years ago, and we haven't spoken since then."

From the corner of her eye, Rachel saw that Nucia had stopped embroidering her father's prayer shawl and had turned her head in their direction to listen. Her mother's head was still bent down as she sewed, as though she wanted no part of this conversation.

"What kind of disagreement?" asked Rachel carefully. Her father didn't mention his parents often.

He cleared his throat before answering in a slow, measured voice. "Zeyde worked in a sweltering brick factory twelve hours a day for wages that barely put food on our plates, and he had this cough—a dry cough that would never go away." He cleared his throat again. "I wanted a different life, a better life away from Gomel, but my father, he wanted me to stay and fight with him for better working conditions. He's never forgiven me for leaving."

Rachel considered this for a moment. "Is Zeyde still working in the brick factory?"

"I don't know."

"Do Zeyde and Bubbe know about Mother, and me and Nucia?"

Her father nodded wearily. "I write them twice a year to let them know how you are."

"You do?" Rachel was surprised and pleased to hear this.

"Yes, but they've never written back to me."

"Oh." Rachel's face fell.

"That's horrible, Father," said Nucia. "I don't think you should write them anymore."

His eyes moved from Rachel to Nucia. "I will not stop writing," he said. "I cannot give up hope that one day they'll forgive me and want to meet all of you. It is my dream for all of us to be together."

Rachel stood and moved around the table to her father. "I'm sure they'll forgive you soon," she said, though she wasn't sure of anything anymore. "You must keep writing."

He pressed his lips together, nodded at Rachel, and gazed out the window.

Rachel moved from the sofa to the samovar, poured herself a glass of tea, and stood beside her father. It was a gray day, with all the color washed out of the sky. In the courtyard, Mr. Berlatsky, Mr. Grienschpoun, and Mr. Nissenson huddled together, smoking and gesturing excitedly with their hands. A halo of smoke hung overhead.

"I think I'll go and join the other men," said her father.

"Can I come?" asked Rachel.

"You stay here with your sister and mother. We'll be talking about grown-up things, not for a young girl's ears." He grabbed his tobacco pouch, put on his coat, and tied the sash.

"Father, I'm not a young girl. I'm almost fifteen, you know!"

Her father turned and smiled at Rachel.

"I know you're a young lady, but you must remain inside." He placed his hand gently on her cheek for a moment and smiled.

When the door shut behind her father, the room seemed to grow colder. Rachel turned and looked at her mother and Nucia. They were absorbed in their sewing and embroidering, their needles moving swiftly through muslin. Rachel quietly picked her black shawl off the hook, slipped on her boots, and opened the door.

Outside the air was brisk and refreshing, like ice-cold tea in the summer. Spying a nearby snow fort built by the Berlatsky children, Rachel waited in the lengthening shadows until she was sure none of the men were looking in her direction. Then she crept over to the fort as quietly as she could and tilted her head in the direction of the men.

"What do you make of the latest article, Gofsha?" said Mr. Nissenson, a tall man with dark black whiskers. "The one in the *Bessarabetz* that says the Rybachenko boy's death was not a ritual murder."

Rachel's father lit his pipe. "Krushevan's words are too late. The damage is done. Fear is rampant among gentiles." He spoke confidently, with authority, so that the other men hung on his words.

Rachel watched her breath spin and disappear into the air. She wiggled her toes and fingers to keep warm.

"This is a curse," said Mr. Nissenson. "And it's bringing shame to all of us here in Kishinev."

"I have more bad news for you," said her father. "These rumors have spread beyond our city. The Petersburg newspaper,

Novoe Vremia, not only had a story about this killing, but it also falsely reported that the Jew who killed Mikhail has already been found."

"We're the chosen people," said Mr. Nissenson. "It's no wonder the whole world is out to get Jews. They envy us."

"How can you believe in such rubbish?" said Rachel's father. "That kind of talk will only lead to more trouble."

"I agree, Gofsha," said Mr. Berlatsky. "But it's hard not to feel like pawns up against a field of kings and queens. The Moldavians hate us for settling on their land, and the peasants hate us for doing better than them."

"That's true. And the newspaper has helped their cause, publishing lie upon lie about us," said Mr. Nissenson.

"That Krushevan is a lowdown good for nothing," said Mr. Grienschpoun in a fierce voice. "I'd like to burn his printing press, and him along with it."

Rachel cowered in fear behind the fort. She had *never* heard Mr. Grienschpoun speak so angrily. He sounded like he wanted to go to war against this Krushevan person. She shivered and hugged herself to stay warm.

"That would prove we're as bad as he says," said her father. "We must keep to ourselves and show that we are honorable, law-abiding citizens."

"Look where that's gotten us," scoffed Mr. Berlatsky. "I think we need to do something to protect our children and ourselves."

"What can we do? We have no power in Kishinev, nobody in government on our side," said Mr. Nissenson in a voice that rose with every word. "The gentiles have occupied all of Russia for years. We are exiles in our own country."

Mr. Berlatsky threw his cigarette butt in Rachel's direction. She hid further back behind the fort and held her breath.

"Who is telling Krushevan these lies?" asked Mr. Berlatsky.

Her father removed his pipe from his mouth. "In the article I read in the *Bessarabetz*, the reporter talked to the man who runs the postal station, and then he paid Mikhail Rybachenko's grandfather to talk about the boy's disappearance."

"But this is crazy! What does the postal man know about what happened to the boy?" Mr. Grienschpoun was practically screaming at Rachel's father.

"How do I know? I'm just telling you what I read."

"I feel bad for the Rybachenkos, but how can they possibly know their grandson's fate?" said Mr. Berlatsky.

"I've heard that a group of rabbis and doctors is going to approach Governor von Raben," said Rachel's father. "Perhaps they'll have some luck in stopping these rumors."

"I wouldn't bet my life on it. I've heard that von Raben prefers gambling to governing," said Mr. Berlatsky. "I'm going in now. I need a glass of vodka to warm my insides."

"Be quiet, unobtrusive, blend into the background, and the worst will pass," warned Rachel's father. "We have a large community here, a strong police force, and almost ten thousand soldiers in the province. I'm sure this will all blow over as soon as the murderer is found."

"I hope you're right," said Mr. Nissenson. "But I'm not counting on it."

Rachel remained in her hiding place as the men said goodbye to one another. She had to wait until her father went inside and then she would pretend she was returning from a visit to the outhouse.

"Are you coming?"

Rachel looked up at the sound of her father's voice. He was leaning over the fort with a bemused expression on his face.

"Are you coming inside?" he asked again. "We're finished out here. There's no more for you to hear."

"I'm sorry Father, I just…I didn't want to embroider with Mother and Nucia, and I didn't want to read, so I…" Her cheeks blazed with embarrassment at being caught.

"You shouldn't have disobeyed me," he said. "Our discussion was not for you to hear."

"Why? Aren't I affected by these rumors? Isn't that what you said? Why shouldn't I hear what's going on?"

"Because I don't want you to worry needlessly. Hopefully, nothing more will happen and we can go back to living on friendly terms with the gentiles. Come, let's go in. Mother will need your help with supper."

Rachel took her father's hand. She glanced at his face as he opened the door. He looked older than usual, and exhausted. New lines cut across his face, wrinkling his skin, and his hair was grayer around the temple. It was as if he had aged overnight, edging one step closer to the end of his life.

❄❄❄

"Ooohh!" Sergei groaned when something fell onto his chest. He opened his eyes gradually, not wanting to let go of slumber.

"Wake up, Sergei. Don't be a lazy slugabed!" Natalya sat on top of him, beating his face playfully with the branch she'd decorated. "The rod beats, beats to tears. I beat thee not, the rod beats!" She sang the traditional Palm Sunday words out, loud and clear.

"It's still dark. I'm tired. Leave me alone." Sergei turned over, jostling his sister, and closed his eyes again.

"But it's Palm Sunday! You can't stay asleep! Only one more week until Easter and the end of Lent. And we get to decorate eggs today. Come! Let's go wake Mama and Papa."

Sergei groaned and pushed Natalya off him. He yawned and slowly sat up, his eyes heavy, his mouth dry and sour from sleep.

"I can hardly wait until you're older and sleep in later," he said.

"Papa told me you once woke him up at four o'clock in the morning on Palm Sunday. I've never gotten up *that* early."

The cold, hard floor on his bare feet jolted Sergei awake. Natalya grabbed his hand and pulled him to their parents' small bedroom adjacent to the living area. They were sound asleep under their feather-filled cover.

"It's Palm Sunday!" Natalya shouted. She threw Sergei her branch and jumped onto their father.

"Oooof." Sergei's father grunted and opened one eye under his bushy brow.

"Beat Papa with the branch! Come on Sergei!" cried Natalya.

"Mercy!" Sergei's mother sat up and looked at them with a startled expression. Her hair, usually pulled back neatly in a braid, fell in every direction, partially covering her plump face. "What's going on? What time is it?"

Sergei, standing at the foot of his parent's bed, squinted to see the time on the wall clock. "Five thirty."

“Good heavens! It’s still the middle of the night.” His mother brushed the hair out of her half-opened eyes with her hand.

“But it’s Palm Sunday, Mama!” Natalya sat on her father’s stomach, her eyes shining.

Sergei’s father put his arms around Natalya and sat up. “Shall I put wood in the stove and fire up the samovar?” He gave her an affectionate smile that made Sergei stiffen with jealousy.

“Yes!” Natalya clapped her hands, scrambling down from the bed.

❄❄❄

Sergei dragged his feet along as he followed his family to the cathedral. In his pocket, he wrapped his hand around the egg Natalya had dyed red. He hoped it wouldn’t crack or break before he gave it to the priest. As he felt the smooth, delicate egg, he wondered what the priest did with the hundreds of eggs he’d receive from families today.

“Tomorrow the whole market will be filled with people selling eggs,” said Natalya. “Mama, how many eggs can we buy this year?”

“Well, I suppose we’ll need some for our Easter dinner, some to give away to people we know…four dozen would probably do.”

“How about six or seven dozen?”

“Why do we need so many eggs?” asked Sergei. “We don’t even have six dozen friends.”

“I want to dye hundreds of eggs and give one to every person I see!” Natalya clapped her hands joyfully.

"That's very generous of you, Natalya." Sergei's father smiled. "But I think four dozen will be enough."

Sergei and his family joined the massive crowd making its way through the door to the Palm Sunday service. As his body was thrust forward, Sergei wiped perspiration from his brow and pulled at his collar.

"Welcome, one and all, to our community, our *sobornost*." The priest stood with his back to the congregation and spoke in a voice as deep as rumbling thunder. "It's Branch Sunday, a special day for our children, but also for our entire congregation. Today we start gathering eggs for Easter Sunday. These eggs symbolize Christ's Resurrection, the most important event in our history, which we'll celebrate in one week. Let us pray."

As he bowed his head, Sergei thought about Mikhail and wondered if he was in heaven with his parents. He tried to imagine another world for people when they died, but he couldn't picture it. It all seemed so unreal, like a place out of the fairy tales he'd heard when he was younger, where animals talked and snow maidens lived in ice castles.

The priest's words fell around him, meaningless and empty, like rain on a hot summer's day that dried as soon as it landed. As he listened, Sergei had trouble breathing and his head pounded. He needed to get out of the crowd before he suffocated. He turned around and used his shoulders to push his way through the people.

"Where are you going, Sergei?" hissed his father. "Get back here now."

"I'm not feeling well," Sergei mouthed back. "I need air."

He ignored countless angry glares and headed for the doorway. When he was finally outside, he breathed a sigh of relief and started walking in the direction of lower Kishinev. Without their cloak of snow, the buildings were even more decrepit than he recalled. One market's walls were cracked and the olive-green paint was peeling. The sagging roof of a bakery looked like it would collapse at any moment.

As soon as he walked into Rachel's courtyard, he felt like an outcast. There were a number of rickety buildings around the perimeter of the courtyard: the largest was a house with a low, tiled roof and windows that couldn't be more than twelve inches wide; the smallest included two outhouses and two sheds. At the far corner was a shop with an outdoor counter made of wooden boxes. A man with a long white beard and a tall black hat leaned against it. He peered at Sergei.

A group of women near a cart of wet clothes stopped talking when he entered and stared at him. Sergei paused and seriously considered turning around. Then he thought about Rachel, and approached the women with a boldness he didn't know he possessed.

"Can you tell me where I might find Rachel?" he asked, his eyes grazing the women's scarf-framed faces. They all wore long, dark skirts in varying shades of black and brown, and threadbare shawls.

"Do you know her?" asked a heavy-set woman.

"Yes."

Silence. Another woman, her red hair arranged in a tidy braid down her back, came forward and stood directly in front of Sergei. She was short—her head came only to Sergei's chest. But the strength in her green eyes belied her stature.

"I'm Rachel's mother," she said with an undertone of impatience. "What do you want with her?"

"I'm a friend. My name is Sergei."

"You stopped those girls from beating her?"

"Yes."

"Thank you."

She turned and entered a house that had eight front doors and four chimney flues. The walls were blistered and rotting, a dark contrast to the beautiful violin music escaping from the window, the passionate strains of Tchaikovsky.

"Has she gone to get Rachel?" Sergei asked the remaining women who were gaping at him. Nobody replied. The violin music stopped and the door opened. Rachel emerged with her mother. She walked over to him with a nervous expression that made him question if he should have come. Her mother stood closely beside her.

"What are you doing here?" Rachel asked him. She wore the same clothes he had seen her in when she was attacked by those girls.

"I…I just really wanted to see you, to talk to you again." He looked up at the women, now eyeing him with suspicion, and lowered his voice. "Can you go for a walk with me?"

She pulled a black shawl tighter around her shoulders and turned her head toward her mother, who nodded. "Yes, I can go for a short time. But only in lower Kishinev."

He followed her onto the street and breathed a sigh of relief at being out of that repressive courtyard. "Was that you playing the violin?"

She laughed. "That was my father. He's tried to teach me but I'm hopeless. My fingers cannot move like his."

"He plays very well."

"I know. He can't read music, but he can play whatever he

hears. It's remarkable."

Sergei shook his head. "I can read music but I can't play a note. Strange."

She nodded.

"How've you been?" he asked as they strolled along the almost-deserted street. Some Jewish men with long whiskers had gathered on the corner, talking to each other in a language he did not understand, their voices converging into one as Rachel and Sergei walked by.

Rachel furrowed her brow and looked straight ahead. "Better, I suppose," she said. "And you?"

Sergei bit his lip. "Not very good."

She tilted her head to look at him. "Why?"

His eyes roamed around, taking in the unfamiliar Jewish quarter. A cabinet shop. A shoemaker's shop. A school with cracks in the walls. The few people they passed walked with heads down to avoid conversation or eye contact.

"Since I saw what happened to you, I've noticed how badly you're all treated. Even my friends are going after Jews, as if it's a game." The words poured quickly from his mouth once he began speaking. "Everyone I know is sure that a Jew killed Mikhail, but there's no proof—just rumors that are getting out of control. I'm afraid my father will never find the real killer because of the lies that are getting in the way of his investigation."

He glanced at Rachel and stopped. Her face was twisted into a portrait of agony. Sergei took her arm and guided her to a more private spot behind a large fir tree.

"What's wrong?" he asked. "I didn't mean to upset you."

Rachel sniffed and wiped the tears from her cheeks. "It's not you," she said quietly. She looked up at Sergei and took a deep breath. "I know who killed Mikhail. I saw everything."

Her words echoed through his ears. "What?"

"I went back for my shawl and saw Mikhail with two big men. He called one 'uncle.'" She paused and looked right into Sergei's eyes. "This uncle, he was a policeman. I recognized his uniform."

The color drained from Sergei's face. The idea of a policeman killing Mikhail was almost too much to bear.

Rachel cleared her throat. "While Mikhail was lying on the ice, the uncle pulled out a knife and stabbed him. The other man, I think I heard Mikhail call him Philip, he kicked Mikhail as he lay there in his own blood."

Sergei clutched his head and paced back and forth trying to make sense of Rachel's words. "Are you *sure*?" he asked her. "That's *exactly* what you saw?"

She nodded, tears streaming down her face. "I was afraid to tell anybody because it was a policeman. I was afraid the police would come after me and my family if I told. What choice did I have if I wanted my family to be safe?"

"But you're telling me now..."

"I want *you* to know the truth, that we are not to blame." She paused and wiped her eyes. "You were Mikhail's closest friend. You deserve to know the truth."

He lifted her chin with his hand so that her eyes met his. "I always knew the rumors were false." His hand dropped to her shoulder.

They stood, face-to-face, for a long time, saying nothing. Sergei felt closer to Rachel at this moment than he had ever felt to anyone else. He knew that he had to do something to put an end to the false stories, and to gain Rachel's trust.

"I will tell my father," he said.

"But—"

"I won't tell him who saw the murder; I promise I'll find a way to tell him about the uncle without putting your family in danger."

Rachel looked up at him with such relief and gratitude, his heart felt like it was going to explode. He drew her closer and wrapped her in his arms. She fit snugly into his embrace.

"I don't know how to thank you," she said a moment later, pulling away from him.

He let go of her and smiled. "I want this whole thing to end as much as you do."

Rachel grimaced. "I want that also, but I'm afraid that even when the truth comes out, Jews and gentiles will never be able to live comfortably beside one another again." She rubbed her hands together. "The words written about us, they cannot be taken back. People will always remember those lies."

Sergei frowned. "I hope you're wrong."

"I should get back home now," she said, turning and heading toward the street.

He nodded and put his hands in his pockets. "Wait! Rachel..." Sergei caught up to her and pulled her red shawl from his coat. "I think this is yours."

Her mouth opened wide when she saw it. "Where..."

"I found it on the ground by the river and remembered seeing it on you. I took it because I didn't want my father or another policeman finding it and coming to the wrong conclusion."

Rachel took the shawl and hugged it to her cheek. "You always believed in me. I won't ever forget what you have done for me and my family."

❄❄❄

"Sit down. You're making me nervous standing over me like that." Sergei's father reached for his cigarette and inhaled. In the last few days his eyes had become swollen, with extra folds of skin underneath.

Sergei perched on the edge of a chair, across the sitting room from his father. It was late. His mother, sister, and aunt had already gone to bed.

"Papa," he began. "I know who killed Mikhail."

His father froze, the cigarette in his hands midway between his mouth and the table. "What did you say?"

Sergei took a deep breath and continued. "Someone I know saw the whole thing. He was at the river that day and saw Mikhail's uncle and cousin Philip attack Mikhail with a knife."

His father exhaled thin streams of smoke. "Why would Mikhail's own uncle want him dead, hmm?"

"I'm not sure…Mikhail hardly ever mentioned his uncle or cousin."

"I see," said Sergei's father. "And why didn't this witness come to the police right away with this story?"

"She…I mean *he* was afraid."

"Why?"

Sergei took a deep breath and prayed his father would believe and accept what he had to say. "The uncle is a policeman. The witness didn't want to put himself or his family in danger."

His father leaner forward. "Sergei, do you know what this is?"

"What?"

"A convenient story made up by a Jew to distract us from

them. Don't you see? This person approached you because you're my son. Whoever he is, he knew you would tell me."

Sergei's heart started racing. "No, Papa. I know the person who told me. I trust him. He would never make up a story like that."

"Oh, Sergei," scoffed his father. "Sometimes I find it hard to believe you're my son. How could you fall for such rubbish?"

"But—"

"You had better learn to tell the difference between the truth and lies before you become a police officer. Or you're going to find yourself on the wrong end of the stick."

Sergei stood up and glared at his father. "I'm *never* going to be a police officer. Never." He ran to his room and wondered how he would tell Rachel that his plan had failed. That his father was so sure a Jew killed Mikhail, he wouldn't even consider another possibility.

APRIL

There was an international-conspiracy meeting in the Kishinev Shul. We need to stand together to beat the Jews over the Easter Holidays.

—Bessarabetz, *April 2, 1903*

One

"Why, on this night, do we only eat matzah?" asked Rachel, looking around the table.

It was the Passover Seder and the Paskar family, along with Sacha and his father, were gathered around the candle-lit table to remember how the Jews fled from slavery in Egypt. Rachel, as the youngest person at the table, had to ask the four important questions about the purpose of the Seder.

"We only eat matzah because our ancestors could not wait for their bread to rise when they were fleeing slavery," answered Sacha in Hebrew. Though the answers were the same every year, Rachel found herself in awe of her ancestors' strength. "They took the bread out of the oven when it was flat."

She continued asking the questions, with Sacha giving the explanations—they were eating a bitter herb to remind themselves of slavery; they were dipping celery in salt water to symbolize the replacing of tears with gratefulness; and they had goose-down pillows on their chairs to sit comfortably, because in ancient times, people who reclined with ease were free from slavery.

Rachel picked up her copy of the *Hagaddah,* and, along with everyone else, read the ten plagues that forced the Egyptians to allow the Jews to escape. Then each person dipped a finger in their cup of wine and spilled a drop on their white plates for every plague—blood, frogs, vermin, wild beasts, pestilence, boils, hail, locusts, darkness, and the slaying of the first born.

Gazing at the stains on her plate, Rachel was reminded that when other people suffer, joy is diminished. She thought about how she hadn't felt good inside since Mikhail's death, and she had trouble keeping her mind on the Seder as she drank the second of four cups of wine, washed her hands, and recited the blessing.

As the fourth cup of wine was poured a few hours later, toward the end of the meal, Mr. Talansky opened the door to welcome in the prophet Elijah. Rachel's father poured an extra cup of wine for Elijah, but while everyone else said a blessing, Rachel couldn't keep her eyes off the open door. She was afraid that at any moment an angry Russian would come rushing through the door waving a sharp knife.

Rachel's father ended the Seder with the traditional words: *Le shana ha-ba'ah b'Yerushalayim*—next year in Jerusalem. Listening to her father's sober tone, Rachel considered the irony of the Seder, how it celebrated the miracle that allowed evil to pass over Jewish homes and spare those people who would have otherwise perished. Now, here they were, thousands of years later, hoping for another miracle to end the hostility in Kishinev without further violence.

Two

"I can't remember when we've had nicer weather for Easter Sunday," said Sergei's mother when she reached the sidewalk. "Last year there was wet snow and it was much colder."

"I remember, Mama," said Natalya. "My hair and bonnet were soaking wet by the time we got home from church."

"Oh, just look at how nice everyone looks…and the colors. It's so nice to see bright colors after such a dull winter. I really feel as if there's a festival today."

Sergei watched the townspeople his mother was talking about, laughing and walking happily on their way home from church. Women were dressed in their best silks, embroidered with silver and gold thread, and they wore tall, elaborate, velvet headdresses.

"I think those headpieces look ridiculous," mumbled Sergei. "I don't feel like celebrating anything today."

His mother shook her head. "That's enough, Sergei. Let's

go to the square. I want to enjoy this lovely weather."

"I just want to go home," said Sergei.

"We are going to the square, as your mother wishes, and that's final." His father beamed at his mother. He signaled to a two-person carriage, pointed to Sergei and Natalya, and then motioned for another carriage for himself and Sergei's mother.

Sergei, with cold gripping his chest, got into the carriage after his sister. Natalya, grinning, put her tiny arm through his. When they reached Chuflinskii Square, there were children playing games at some of the outdoor booths, while adults sat at tables drinking beer and vodka.

"Papa," said Natalya, "why is the merry-go-round not moving?"

Sergei looked at the center of the square and saw that the carousel was, indeed, silent and still.

"The Ministry of Interior has decided that amusements like the merry-go-round should not open on holidays," Sergei's father replied.

"What a shame," said Sergei's mother, brushing her hand over Natalya's hair. "The square seems odd without the carousel music."

Sergei stared at the motionless carousel horses and felt as if a shadow was hanging over the square, as if life was about to change forever.

The sound of breaking glass, followed by a woman's piercing scream, diverted Sergei's attention from the merry-go-round. Turning toward the noise, he saw a group of men and boys throwing glasses at an elderly Jewish woman.

"Let's have some fun with the Jews!" they shouted. They wore long, red, belted blouses, and their pants were tucked into tall boots. Sergei could tell by their staggering gait that they had been drinking.

The church bells pealed, announcing the noon hour.

"Go home, all of you." Sergei's father moved briskly toward the group of men.

"There's no law against being outdoors," said a bulky man in a slurred voice.

"That's right." A few other people voiced their displeasure at being ordered to leave, turned their backs on Sergei's father, and kept drinking.

"Keep it down," ordered Sergei's father in his authoritative police chief voice. "We're going to have extra police working this weekend, so watch yourselves or you'll end up in jail." He stood behind the men for a moment, as if he was expecting a response, and then walked back to his family. "Those men are big with noise but short of brains," he said. "They'll be passed out before they can do any real harm. Come—" He held out his right arm to Sergei's mother, who grasped it with both hands. "Let's enjoy this fine day."

Sergei watched his sister take hold of his father's other arm. The three of them paraded down the square as if nothing was the matter. Sergei scowled and sat down on a bench. He exhaled when he saw the Jewish woman run safely out of the square, but grew anxious when the men resumed their boisterous drinking. He could feel the tension in the air, sense the doom that was coming, and was disgusted by his own uselessness. Without anyone fighting the tide of hatred, he could not even begin to hope for a good outcome. Perhaps Nikolai was right, he fretted, about something bad happening this weekend.

"Beat the Yids!"

Sergei's jaw dropped when he saw at least twenty-five people, mostly men, surrounding another Jewish woman.

"Stop!" she cried. "Somebody help me!"

Sergei stood up and looked across the square at his father as the crowd chased the woman, screaming "Beat the Yids!" over and over. He ran toward his family and saw his sister and mother hanging onto his father.

"I need to get some more officers down here," said his father, plucking Natalya and his wife's hands off his torso. "Take the children home, Tonia. I'm going back to the station."

"Papa! Papa, you have to stop those people now," cried Sergei, "before someone gets hurt."

"I'm not risking my life to stop those idiots. Go home with your mother."

Sergei winced when he saw a Jewish man being taunted mercilessly, while a group of young men chased a Jewish boy.

"Papa, you have to do something!"

"I'm not going to tell you again. Leave the police work to me and stop worrying about the Jews." Sergei's father walked away without looking back.

"Please come, Sergei," pleaded Natalya.

Sergei gazed at his sister's frightened face. "You go with Mama," he told her. "I'll come soon."

He headed out of the square, his ears burning with the sound of his sister's cries mixed with raging voices yelling obscenities at the Jews. He put his hands over his ears, but the sound grew with every minute. He lowered his hands and quickened his pace.

Large crosses were chalked on many store windows, and in others icons hung in plain view. Sergei realized these shop owners wanted to make it clear that they were not Jewish, as if they had sensed approaching danger. Up ahead, he saw boys and men throwing rocks at shops without crosses or icons.

Sergei looked frantically for police officers but couldn't find even one. As he got closer to lower Kishinev, he saw boys whistling, shouting, and throwing rocks as they marched. Behind them, men carried crowbars, smashing Jewish shops and homes along the street. Women and men stood at the side of the road cheering the rioters on. Some were stealing items from Jewish stores that had been vandalized. Others dressed themselves in layers of clothes they took from the demolished stores.

The noise pounded inside Sergei's head. He wanted everything to disappear, but it just got louder and louder.

Hearing a carriage coming from behind him, Sergei turned, hoping to see the police. But it was Bishop Iakov's carriage. Sergei assumed the bishop would put an end to the violence, but the regal man, dressed in his gold-trimmed vestments, simply waved to the bystanders and continued on his way. People cheered as he moved past them. Sergei stood in shock for a moment, unable to move. If the bishop didn't put a stop to this, he wondered, what hope did the Jews have?

The crowd was moving toward lower Kishinev. Rachel could be in danger. Sergei started running in the direction of her house and didn't stop until he was in Rachel's courtyard.

"A gezunt dir in pupik!"

"What?" Sergei looked at the man who had spoken. He was wearing a tattered robe and had so many wrinkles on his face his skin looked as though it might crack open.

"He's saying good health to your belly button." Sergei turned around and saw Rachel standing in front of her doorway. Her face was pale and strained. "He says the same thing to everyone. He's been strange ever since he lost his job." She closed the door behind her and stepped toward him.

"Rachel, you have to stay inside. There's a riot going on in town. Peasants are bashing Jewish stores and homes with crowbars and rocks."

"Oh no!" she covered her mouth with her hand. "Haven't you told your father yet, about Mikhail's uncle?"

Sergei gulped and averted his eyes. "Yes. I did, but he wouldn't listen. He wants only to believe that a Jew is guilty."

Rachel's face fell. "I should have said something earlier. I should have gone to the police myself."

"Then you might have been hurt—or your family. It's clear to me now that the simple truth is no match for the lies printed in the newspaper."

"What are we going to do if the rioters come here? We have nowhere else to go."

Sergei chewed his bottom lip and thought about what to say to make Rachel feel better. "I know there are extra policemen on duty this weekend. Hopefully they'll have everything under control soon. Just stay inside and tell your father." Sergei's face turned red. He had to look down at his boots in order to get the rest of his words out. "I...I don't want anything to happen to you."

She nodded, backed into her doorway, and disappeared.

Sergei stared at her house. "Stay safe, Rachel," he whispered, before running home.

❄❄❄

"…get hurt…stay with us…"

"Don't worry…many are coming…"

Rachel woke to her parents' agitated voices. She got off her bench and pulled aside the muslin curtain. Except for a lit oil lamp on the table, the house was swathed in darkness. Sunday night had not yet given way to Monday morning.

Her father was tying the sash on his overcoat, while her mother stood nearby, clutching a square of white muslin.

"Father, where are you going?" The sight of him getting ready to leave so early alarmed Rachel.

His hands shook as he put his black *yarmulka* on his head. "A group of us are going to the New Marketplace."

Rachel ran over to her father and wrapped her arms around him. "But Sergei said they had crowbars and were throwing rocks at Jews there yesterday. You could get hurt." She sobbed into his coat. "Don't go, Father. Please don't go!"

"Even your daughter knows better than you today," said her mother.

He pushed Rachel back firmly and looked into her eyes. "I must go to see what happened last night. The Talanskys live near there." He cleared his throat. "Don't you want me to see if they need help?"

Rachel lowered her eyes. "I suppose so…but Father—"

Her father smiled grimly and hugged Rachel. "Nothing's going to happen to me."

"Promise?"

"I promise." He walked over to Rachel's mother, kissed her on the cheek, and held her hand for a moment.

"Do not leave the house today," he ordered Rachel, before

closing the door. "We want to make sure the riots are over before you go outside again. And be good for your mother."

She kept her eyes on the door after it closed behind her father, hoping he would change his mind and reappear. But the door stayed shut, solid and forbidding.

❄❄❄

Rachel picked at her matzah and dates and watched Nucia sweep the floor. "You know you've been sweeping the same spot for thirty minutes," she said to her sister in a listless voice.

"I don't care." Nucia gripped the broom tightly in her hands as she swept.

Rachel looked at her mother washing dishes and then at the small clock hanging on the wall beside the door. Almost ten o'clock. "Father's been gone nearly four hours. When will he be back?"

"How should I know? Am I there? He'll be home when he's home. Now eat."

She put a piece of matzah in her mouth. It tasted extra dry, and the more she chewed, the more there seemed to be in her mouth. An unexpected knock at the door caused the matzah to slip down her throat, making her gag.

Her mother opened the door. The young policeman who had questioned Rachel before stood outside.

"There's, um, trouble in the New Marketplace. You'd best not go out of your home," he said. "We don't, um, want you to get hurt."

"What's going on?" cried her mother. "Gofsha, my husband, is there as we speak."

Rachel ran over to the door. "He went with some other men to help."

The policeman frowned. "He shouldn't have gone." He put his hand to his forehead, gritted his teeth, and exhaled. "I have orders to stay here today, but if I hear anything about the marketplace I'll, um, let you know."

"Thank you very much," said Rachel's mother. She locked the door and stood perfectly still for a moment. Then she took a deep breath and poured herself another glass of tea.

Nucia fell to the floor and cried softly, still clutching the broom. Rachel's mother began scouring the walls with a rag, scrubbing as if she was trying to wipe the surface off.

"Father will be all right. He promised me," Rachel assured them, sounding more confident than she felt. She twisted her braid with her hand as she stood at the window and waited for her father to return.

She could not take her eyes off the courtyard, which was eerily quiet and empty. The old gray-cement courtyard walls looked filthy and shabby against the perfectly clear blue sky. The policeman was pacing back and forth on the street, which made her feel a bit safer. Nobody would dare enter their courtyard and start destroying the houses with a policeman on guard, would they?

"Come, Rachel," said her mother an hour later. "You must eat something. Nucia and I are having some bread and butter."

"I'm not hungry," she said, without turning away from the window. Her stomach was cramped from anxiety. Every minute that passed seemed like an hour. She chewed on her hair to pass the time.

Shadows from trees on the street began to dance on the

courtyard walls. The sun was going down without any sign of her father. Rachel turned and looked at her mother and sister. They were sitting in front of the stove knitting, their needles moving rapidly through the red wool.

"How can you sit there as if nothing's the matter?" Rachel cried.

"Worrying never helps," her mother answered in a flat voice, hands still flying smoothly through the air. "You have stood by that window all day and what good has it done?"

"But at least..." Rachel stopped speaking when she heard the door creak open. "He's home! Father's home!" She threw herself into her father's arms.

"Gofsha, we were so frightened," said Rachel's mother. "How grateful I am that you're safe."

A smile spread across Nucia's face. She dropped her knitting and ran over to give him a big hug.

"The policeman was here, Father," said Rachel. "He said things were getting worse in town."

Her father sat down wearily by the stove and stared into the fire. His face and clothing were smeared with dirt. He was breathing heavily and gray pouches hung under his bloodshot eyes.

"It's...the worst...I've ever seen," he said in a halting, breathless voice. "There must have been about...a hundred of us. We were able...to stop a small group of people...from ruining a store." He cleared his throat. "But the police arrived...and ordered us home. They even arrested...a couple of men who... wanted to stay and protect their shops from rioters."

"What are we going to do, Gofsha?" cried Rachel's mother.

Rachel shrank back from her family, overwrought with

guilt. She wished, more than ever, that she had gone to the police right away. Then maybe only she would be in danger, not every Jew in town.

"Now listen to me," said Rachel's father, his voice gaining strength with every word. "You must all do exactly as I say." He stood, marched over to the window, and peered out. Then he closed and latched the wooden shutter. "You're all going to hide in the outhouse with the Grienschpouns. Until this is over. To be safe."

Rachel could hardly breathe. "Do you really think they'll come here?" she asked her father.

"I don't know. We came home as quickly as we could, but we heard people behind us yelling out, 'stupid, dirty Yids.' We must not take any chances."

"What about Chaia and her family?" asked Rachel.

"They're going to hide in the shed," her father replied. "There's more room for them there."

"This can't be happening," said Nucia in a weak, raspy voice. Her face was ashen gray. "I think I'm going to be sick." She held her abdomen and groaned.

Rachel's father bent down, hugged Nucia, and pulled her to her feet. "Hurry—there's no time to take anything with you. Go now. Before they get here." He pushed Nucia to the door and gestured for Rachel and her mother to follow.

"What about you? Aren't you coming too?" asked Rachel, when she saw that her father wasn't following them. "I don't want to go anywhere without you, Father."

"I'll come as soon as I make sure all the people in our house are safe. Now shut the door before the rioters arrive in our courtyard."

Rachel entered the crude, weathered outhouse with her mother and sister. Mrs. Grienschpoun, a buxom woman with rosy cheeks, and her two red-haired little boys were already sitting on the bench that ran along one wall. Mr. Grienschpoun was placing a couple of old wood planks over the two holes in the other bench that opened to the ground. His bright red hair and whiskers seemed out of place in the drab outhouse.

Snow had seeped through the edges where the walls and floor met, leaving the ground wet and partially covered with snow. The strong smell was almost overpowering.

"We all need to be absolutely quiet," whispered Mr. Grienschpoun. "Remember, the door doesn't lock from the inside."

"Then why are we hiding here?" asked Rachel.

"Because there's nothing to break or steal, so hopefully they won't even think of coming in. I'm going to see that everyone else is well hidden. Stay here and keep quiet." He opened the door slowly and ran out. Mrs. Grienschpoun and her children began crying softly as they huddled in the corner.

Rachel's mother and sister sat down on the board set in place by Mr. Grienschpoun. Rachel cleared a corner by kicking the snow away, sat down, closed her eyes, and prayed for her father to come through the door soon.

"Have mercy and pity on us," she whispered. "Please, protect us all."

For a few minutes, silence was their only companion. Then the terrifying clamor of people marching and screaming began, growing louder and louder until it sounded as if they were right outside the outhouse. Rachel sat frozen in place, terrified at the thought of the outhouse door being ripped open by the rioters.

"Give us thirty rubles or we will kill you," yelled a crowd outside in unison, like students reciting a lesson.

Rachel heard Mr. Serebrenik, the shopkeeper, stammer, "H…here…here, take it." There was silence and then the smash of glass breaking. As the crowd drew nearer, Rachel heard something hitting the stone walls hard and felt her chin quiver in fear.

Masculine voices yelled, "Beat the Yids!"

Cheers rose from the crowd.

Rachel hugged her knees to her chest and tried to bury her head, to drown out the noise. *Crash!* Glass shattered. *Bang! Thump!* Heavy objects fell to the ground. Hearing the sounds of havoc, of destruction, all around her, without being able to see anything terrified Rachel. She held her breath as heavy footsteps ran toward the outhouse, and exhaled when the footsteps moved past their hiding place. "Where's Father?" she mumbled softly.

Seconds later, a powerful bang, like thunder, sounded above them.

"I think someone's on the roof of the outhouse," whispered Rachel to her mother and Nucia.

On the bench, Mrs. Grienschpoun looked up and clung to her two boys tightly.

Rachel listened in horror as two more loud bangs shook the old roof. It wobbled precariously with each collision.

"Ech! The entire roof is going to fall on top of us," Rachel whispered.

Voices rose from the courtyard, cheering the rioters on. Suddenly, there was a massive crash and then a thump.

"Ohh…" A groan from the man on the roof brought laughter from the crowd outside. "Help!"

"That sounded like Mr. Grienschpoun," Nucia said.

"I know." Rachel looked over and saw Mrs. Grienschpoun with her head down and her body trembling as she sobbed noiselessly.

Rachel stood up and crammed herself in beside her mother and Nucia. They clutched each other and listened helplessly to the frightening noises. Shrieks of pain and terror came from above. Rachel closed her eyes and held her hands over her ears to block out the sounds of agony, but it was impossible.

"They're throwing something at him," said Rachel's mother. She looked smaller, a fraction of herself, receding into the outhouse.

"I hope Father's all right," whispered Rachel as she pulled her mother and Nucia closer, trying not to cry out loud.

"Stop!"

Rachel's head shot up when she heard Sergei's voice.

She couldn't believe he was in her courtyard, urging people to stop the violence. Hope warmed her heart as she heard him say, "Enough already…too far…" She couldn't make out all his words because of the noise from the crowd. It was maddening, knowing he was so close to her and yet she could not show herself.

❄❄❄

Sergei saw a mass of people shouting in the street outside Rachel's courtyard. They were beating a man lying in a mud puddle with wooden clubs. When his attackers stepped back, the man asked for water in a feeble voice. Sergei could tell that his legs and arms had been broken in many places from the peculiar way they dangled from his body. A couple of Jewish men lugged him from the puddle, gave him water, and started to wipe the dirt and blood off his face.

"The Yid's still alive!" yelled one of the rioters.

The Jews that were helping the man quickly disappeared into the crowd.

Another rioter veered around and struck the groaning man on the head with a crowbar, knocking him over so he lay face down in the mud. His bony legs shook for a moment and then were still.

As Sergei gaped at the victim, he noticed four police officers huddled together. He elbowed his way frantically through the crowd to reach them.

"Stop them!" Sergei demanded, pointing back at the attackers.

One of the officers shrugged. "Don't have any orders to stop it."

"What are you talking about? Why do you need orders? They're breaking the law, aren't they? Look…they've killed that man over there." Sergei pointed to the man who now lay dead in the mud.

"He's right," said another officer. "If the governor were here, he'd stop them."

"But he's not here," snarled a third. "There's nothing we can do until the governor gives us orders. Why don't you just leave and go home, before *you* get hurt."

"No! How can you just stand there and do nothing? You have to do something. Please!" cried Sergei.

"Look, just go home. By tomorrow this should all be over." Three of the officers sauntered off as casually as if they were walking to a tavern.

The one who remained gave Sergei another shrug, this time looking only mildly apologetic as he sat down on the wooden curb.

Undeterred, Sergei fought his way into Rachel's courtyard—past a handful of raging men hurling sticks and rocks toward the house; past men in ragged clothing waving knives and crowbars, as if in battle; past women and boys hurling insults that scorched the air. Sergei pushed his way toward Rachel's house and was quickly swept up by the throng of people. He found himself staring at the remains of her home—an empty shell with battered windows and doors.

"Stop!" he cried out as he watched men and women discarding the contents of Rachel's life, throwing dishes, mattresses, clothing, and their samovar from the door and windows.

"Stop!" a chorus of voices echoed Sergei.

He listened in disbelief as words of protest rippled through the crowd.

"Enough already!"

"It's gone too far!"

"You're behaving like savage animals!"

He spun around and was amazed to see both Christians and Jews, united in fear, pleading with the rioters to stop. Relief surged through him, sustaining his faith that good could triumph over evil. He cried out with renewed energy and determination for the crowd to help end this unprovoked attack. But tolerance succumbed to rage. Sergei and the other protestors were sorely outnumbered. They could not stop the tortuous killing of a man with bright red hair on top of a rickety outhouse.

❄❄❄

The voice on the roof grew weak. Rachel could tell that the man was unable to keep fighting for himself. There was a big thump, the crowd cheered, and Rachel stared at Nucia in horror. The man had fallen off the roof.

Rachel listened for Sergei's voice, but only wailing, shattering glass, heavy footsteps, and loud bangs filled the tiny outhouse, making it seem smaller and smaller until the walls closed in on them. Her body was cramped from being in one position for so long. She shook her tingling foot. The rioting went on and on as Rachel listened, tense with fear. At any moment, the unlocked door might open. She sniffed the air. Smoke was beginning to seep into the outhouse.

Feeling like she would suffocate, Rachel hugged herself tightly and recited the Eighteen Benedictions in her head, over and over, trying to soothe her fear with familiar Hebrew words.

As the black night darkened the outhouse, the noise subsided. Rachel listened as the crowd dispersed, a low murmur fading away. Her eyes met Nucia's, then her mother's. Nobody in the outhouse moved or spoke. The Grienschpoun boys had fallen into a restless sleep, cradled in their mother's arms. Rachel sank back against the wall, afraid to make a sound, afraid of what awaited all of them outside.

❄❄❄

Sergei rushed into his father's office and found him busy receiving a telegraph. He watched impatiently as his father tapped a reply, tugging at his whiskers as he sent the message. He glanced up at Sergei when he was finished and frowned.

"Papa, have you seen what's going on? A mob of people

has descended on lower Kishinev and is attacking Jews, and the police are doing nothing."

His father stared at him. "Why are you so concerned about lower Kishinev, hmm?"

"I know someone there. A friend. She was Mikhail's friend too. I know he would want me to help her." His father's face tightened as Sergei continued speaking. "You have to order the officers to stop the attacks."

Sergei's father narrowed his eyes so that his brows came together in a V. "I can't give special treatment to someone, just because she's your *friend.* There are three infantry companies and two cavalry squadrons in place, and I will have extra officers on duty all night."

"All night! You think this violence will be going on all night?"

"It's possible."

Sergei smelled alcohol on his breath. "But you can stop it now. You have enough officers."

"We have to wait for orders from the governor." Sergei's father put on his cap and buttoned up his coat.

"What are you talking about?"

"I have to leave now. You're to go home and stay there with your mother and sister. Do you hear me?" He waved his finger in Sergei's face.

"But why do you have to wait for orders?"

"Did you hear me?"

"But—"

"Go. Now!" Sergei's father pointed to the door.

Sergei left, but he didn't go home. Intent on finding Rachel, he started back to lower Kishinev.

By the time Sergei reached Gostinnii Street, he felt as if he was in a completely different city, the damage was so extensive. The Jewish tobacco store was destroyed. The front wall had collapsed, revealing the skeletal remains of the building. Shelves were torn from the walls and cartons had tipped over. Sergei swallowed and moved to the next store, the shoemaker's shop with broken windows and doors beaten until they'd collapsed. Everything inside was gone or vandalized. It got worse as he continued walking. Homes and apartments ransacked. Furniture sitting in the streets, torn apart, broken beyond recognition.

The air reeked of wine, beer, and decay. Sergei stood motionless in front of a wine shop where broken bottles lay strewn across the pavement. He resumed walking, but a minute later stopped again when he saw dead, twisted bodies piled on top of one another in front of a Jewish bookstore. At the very top of the pile was a small boy, his head hanging over the edge, his clothing ripped, his skin a lifeless fish-gray.

Sergei gagged at the putrid stench of burnt flesh and blood, dirt and feathers, which were smeared over the bodies. Covering his mouth, he dashed to the edge of the sidewalk, where he crouched and vomited; he didn't get up until the retching pain in his gut had eased and his legs felt steady.

When Sergei came to a residential street, his heart plummeted. There was no way people could have survived so much destruction. Feathers from pillows covered the ground like a blanket of snow. Pieces of tables, beds, and sofas littered the street.

"Bubbe...Bubbe..."

As Sergei stared at the devastation, he heard a small voice in one of the vandalized houses. Moving closer, he realized there was no longer a door, just a narrow, murky hole. He entered cautiously, following the sound. Sitting behind a wide trunk, which had miraculously survived, was a small boy with messy blond hair and swollen amber eyes sunk back in his face.

The boy stared anxiously at Sergei, trying to press his body against the wall.

"I won't hurt you." Sergei kneeled down to the boy's level. "I'm Sergei. Can you tell me your name?"

The boy sniffed back some tears and wrapped his arms around his knees. "Menahem Katsap."

"How old are you?"

Menahem sniffed. "Seven."

Sergei's brow furrowed. He didn't look more than four or five. "Where's the rest of your family?"

Menahem started sobbing.

"I'm sorry…I'm so sorry." Sergei reached out and gently touched the boy's shoulder.

"My grandmother…was beat up."

"Where is she?"

"I don't know."

"And you lived with her?"

Menahem nodded. Gray mucus dripped from his nose.

"Come with me." Sergei held out his hand. Menahem carefully searched Sergei's face before taking his hand.

"Where are we going?"

"To the hospital. To make sure you're all right. They'll take care of you and we'll see if your grandmother is there."

"Will she be all right?" The little boy trembled as he looked up at Sergei.

"I don't know." Sergei, fearing the worst, couldn't look Menahem in the eye. "Maybe they'll know more at the hospital."

❄❄❄

The Jewish Hospital was located along the slope of Nicolayevskaya Street. It was a substantial two-story building enclosed within a courtyard now crammed with injured people—standing, sitting, and lying unconscious on the muddy ground. As they approached the steps leading inside, Sergei felt Menahem's cold, skinny fingers clutch his hand tighter. Sergei held his breath as he pushed open the hospital's heavy door. Inside, the waiting area, too, was packed with wounded people. Their raw, open sores and grief-stricken eyes made Sergei look away, but he couldn't escape their moaning and the horrid smell of urine, blood, and despair.

"Can I help you?" A nurse greeted Sergei and Menahem in a harried voice. She spoke loudly to be heard above the background commotion. "Just a minute," she said to a man with a bandaged head standing behind her. She looked at Sergei expectantly.

"I found this boy all alone. His name is Menahem Katsap. He says his grandmother was beaten. Maybe she's here waiting for him."

The nurse bent down and spoke gently to Menahem. "Did anybody hurt you?"

Menahem shook his head.

"Would you like to come with me? Perhaps we can take a look at you and find out what happened to your grandmother."

Menahem looked at Sergei, who nodded, then took the nurse's hand.

"Do you know if anyone from the Paskar family is here?" asked Sergei.

The nurse gave him a curious look and examined the chart in her hand. "No, I don't have anyone here with that name, but they could arrive later..."

Sergei nodded and looked down at his shoes, which were covered with mud.

"Thank you," the nurse said, her voice softer and kinder. "For bringing Menahem here."

Sergei put his hand on Menahem's shoulder, then watched them walk down the hall until he couldn't see them anymore. He left, more determined than ever to find Rachel.

Out on the street, Sergei was swept up in a sea of people, mostly men and teenage boys, waving clubs and canes wildly in the air, wearing the same long, red blouses and tall boots he had seen on the men in the square yesterday. The uniform of mass hatred.

A nervous energy ignited the mob when they reached house No. 33 on Gostinnii Street. They surged and attacked, breaking windows and pushing in the door. A few leaders barged into the home, found the residents hiding in the attic, and beat them mercilessly. One man dragged a young boy outside and beat him to death with a crowbar, while the child's father begged for mercy.

Sergei was sick to his stomach again—this time on the sidewalk. He looked around for a policeman but saw none. Breaking away from the boisterous crowd, he ran further south to find help.

Down the street, at house No. 66, another gang of rioters was ambushing a troika driver.

"Can you believe it?" a woman said to Sergei when he stopped beside her. "That idiot Jew driver refused to take that poor boy to the hospital. He died. It's terrible. Just terrible."

Sergei watched, transfixed, as the driver was murdered right in front of him. Clubbed to death. Sergei looked around again for a policeman. Instead, he saw two more men and a young woman being brutally beaten and kicked in the courtyard. Both of the men were unconscious, and the woman was groaning. The crowd was cheering the attackers on.

Sergei ran toward Asia Street and passed the New Bessarabia Hotel, which an angry throng was busy destroying. Grocery stores, bakeries, a wine shop, a jewelry store, and a tavern were all being demolished. Furniture was scattered across the pavement. People were taking whatever they could carry from the ruined stores.

"Stop...you must stop," cried Father Petrov, a young priest. He stood in front of a small house, his black cassock splattered with mud, and pressed his palms out toward the angry rioters. "We must not attack our Jewish neighbors. They are good, honest people."

"How can you defend them, with their crazy blood rituals?" yelled a man waving a crowbar in the air.

"You're wrong," cried Father Petrov fervently. "Jewish people don't eat any meat that has blood in it. This is part of their culture. This idea of consuming blood directly contradicts their religion."

A few people stopped and listened to the priest, their eyebrows rising with comprehension as he spoke. They moved slowly back from the house and the mob. But more of them, Sergei noted, kept going, ignoring the priest's words.

Sergei walked aimlessly, his mind reeling with the horrific sights, smells, and sounds he had experienced. Kishinev had become derelict, dirty, and ravaged overnight. On one corner, three bodies lay together—a woman, man, and boy. He prayed the little boy never felt any pain.

The boy reminded Sergei of Menahem, who had seen his own grandmother beaten, and Natalya, who was so close in age, so vulnerable. Suddenly, he needed to see his sister and his mother, to make sure they were safe. He took off toward upper Kishinev where the streets were cleaner, the violence less apparent. Police seemed to be everywhere. As he passed his school, he noticed clusters of students surrounding the limestone building, discussing the chaos they'd witnessed. Sergei nodded at boys he knew, many of whom looked exhausted and tense.

"Sergei." He heard his name and saw Nikolai striding toward him. "Have you seen the center of Kishinev? The whole city looks like it's been in a war."

Sergei nodded. "I don't think I'll ever forgive my father. He did nothing to stop the fighting."

"My father saw him insulting a bunch of Jews."

"Damm! Where was your father at the time?"

"He was watching the riots."

"Then he's guilty too."

"Of what?"

"Of not stopping the fighting."

"But there were hundreds of people, and he's only one." Nikolai glanced at the group of boys surrounding them. He spotted Petya and spoke to him. "What did your father do last night?"

Petya came forward slowly, his face so pale that his freckles appeared darker than usual. "Well, we were, uh, having dinner… at a friend's house. Then the windows were smashed so we rushed home where we found some peasants about to throw rocks at our windows. My father told them he was the mayor, that it was his house." Petya swallowed. He looked as if he was going to be sick. "So…so they threw rocks at our neighbor's house, the Grossmans. Almost every window was smashed. I could hear Mrs. Grossman scream. She had just brought over a big plate of pastries a day earlier." His eyes were heavy with regret.

Even Petya's father, the mayor, thought Sergei, had been nothing more than a coward in the face of danger. Instead of standing up for what was right, for his own neighbors, he'd led a mob of angry people to their door for certain vandalism…and worse. Sergei now understood what Rachel had meant about trust. If he couldn't depend on his father, or the mayor, or his friends, then who could he trust?

❄❄❄

Rachel's neck was stiff and her head ached. She'd spent the night sitting on the floor of the outhouse, lapsing into brief periods of sleep, then waking suddenly with fear slicing her heart. Nucia's head rested on her sister's shoulder. Her mother sat beside them, dark shadows under her puffy eyes. On the opposite wall, Mrs. Grienschpoun stared blankly at Rachel. Her boys had their arms wrapped around her, and their small faces were stained with dry tears and dirt.

Rachel touched her sister on the shoulder. "Nucia, are you awake?"

"I guess so." Nucia lifted her head and yawned.

The two little boys began squirming when they heard Rachel and Nucia.

"Nucia…Rachel…are you all right?" said their mother.

"Yes," answered Nucia.

"What about Father? Why didn't he come back?" asked Rachel.

There were a few seconds of silence before her mother answered: "I wish I knew."

A chill ran through Rachel's body when she recalled the previous night. The sound of hatred. The smell of death.

"I think we should go outside now," said her mother in a shaky voice. "There's no sense in putting off what must come."

Mrs. Grienschpoun got to her feet, holding her boys close to her. Rachel could not look at the boys' faces. She was afraid they would see her fear.

Clinging tightly to her mother's waist, Rachel opened the door and walked outside; the others followed.

Their courtyard was filled with broken glass and furniture, ripped bedding, torn clothing, and enamel basins. The ground was tarnished with bloody spots that had darkened around the edges. Pages of scripture were scattered everywhere. Feathers from pillows and coverlets draped the trees and ground like a winter's frost. Rachel turned in a full circle and gasped when she saw a man lying dead at the side of the outhouse. It was Mr. Grienschpoun. She could tell by his red hair. His face was unrecognizable, bashed in and covered in blood. His coat was torn, dirty, and stained crimson.

"No!" Rachel screamed and pointed to Mr. Grienschpoun. "Help!"

Mrs. Grienschpoun collapsed on the ground weeping. Her boys clutched at her and cried. Nucia and Rachel's mother knelt down and put their arms around Mrs. Grienschpoun and her sons.

Rachel burst into tears at the sight of the Grienschpouns mourning their dead husband and father. "Where's Father?" she cried. "I want to see Father!" She ran toward her house. Ignoring the destruction, Rachel kept her eyes straight ahead as she ran, stopping only when she came to her house—what remained of her house. Feeling as if she were caught in the middle of one of her bad dreams, she rubbed her eyes to wake up and escape. But this was real, all of it: the terrifying night in the outhouse, Mr. Grienschpoun, and now her decimated home. Though she was trembling, afraid of what she might find, Rachel stepped forward to survey the damage. The window was smashed and the door was gone. Inside, the rioters had poured wine over everything. Furniture was broken, shutters were torn off the walls, ripped clothing was scattered all over the floor, and the remains of her father's precious chess board looked like it had been pounded with a mallet. And Snegurochka was smashed into pieces—only the head was intact. Her journal had been ripped apart, the pages scattered on the ground, exposing her private thoughts for all to see. Although Rachel knew that the Russians who'd destroyed her diary couldn't read Yiddish, she still felt as if she'd been beaten and stripped of her dignity; she knelt down to pick up the pages.

"Who could do such a thing?" Rachel's mother appeared in the doorway, tears sliding down her face. "Everything we owned is gone. We have nothing left. Nothing." She moved to the middle of the room, her face leeched of color, her shoulders sagging with despair.

Rachel had never seen her mother so defeated. This frightened her and made her world seem even more off-balance. She shivered and wondered if the worst was yet to come.

Rachel led them past the other ruined houses in their courtyard, now unrecognizable. When they got to the end of the house and turned the corner toward the street, Rachel cried out a heart-wrenching scream that echoed in the stale air.

On the trampled ground lay Mr. Macklin, the landlord of the house, and Mr. Berlatsky. Their bodies were broken, their limbs bent in impossible directions, and they were covered with mud. Feathers were scattered everywhere. A few feet to the right, Mrs. Berlatsky sat with Chaia's head in her lap. Chaia's eyes were closed but she was moving slightly and groaning, and her beautiful hair was matted with blood. The three other children sat at their mother's feet weeping.

Rachel couldn't speak, and she couldn't take her eyes of Chaia. She felt as if she were watching from afar, that none of this was happening. Chaia had done nothing to deserve this. Neither had Mr. Macklin or Mr. Berlatsky or Mr. Grienschpoun—or their children, now fatherless. Their only shortcoming was their faith, a crime in the eyes of gentiles. Rachel peered at Chaia's listless face, and began to wonder if believing in something you couldn't even see—faith—was worth all the trouble it brought.

"We were hiding in the shed," said Elena Berlatsky a few minutes later. Her voice quivered as she spoke. Nucia put her arms around the two smaller Berlatzky children while her mother and Mrs. Berlatsky sat with Chaia. "When we heard them coming after us, we climbed up to the attic, but it was too hard to move around all the rafters and chimney flues. We could hear them screaming at us, so we tore at the roof with our hands to make a hole to climb through." She paused to sniff and wipe her eyes. "Luckily, the roof had already started to rot. All of us made it up there except for Mr. Macklin and Father. Someone grabbed Mr. Macklin's legs and pulled him down from the attic. Then, when somebody grabbed Father's legs, Chaia lay down on the roof, reached through the hole, and held onto his arms. She pulled as hard as she could to get him on top of the roof, but the person who had Father's legs was much stronger."

Elena's voice began to crack. "Before we knew what had happened, Father was pulled down from the attic with Chaia holding onto him. Then…" Elena looked at Rachel's mother. "Then they dragged them out onto the ground and the crowd beat them with crowbars."

Rachel wept as she heard what Chaia had endured, and she began to panic at the thought of her father lying somewhere in pain, or worse. "I want to see Father," she said in a quiet voice, feeling guilty for thinking about him after hearing about what the Berlatskys had been through.

"Will you be…all right if I…leave for a few minutes?" Rachel's mother asked Mrs. Berlatzky.

Rachel was startled by her mother's meek tone, and by the way her voice faltered. It was almost as if she were a different person.

Mrs. Berlatzky nodded and brushed Chaia's hair out of her face. "I need to get Chaia to the hospital. I couldn't bear to lose—" She burst into tears.

Rachel watched as her mother pressed her lips together but said nothing. Before, thought Rachel, Mother would have said something to make Mrs. Berlatsky feel better. Behind her mother's severe demeanor was a woman who would do anything for the people she cared for. Looking back, Rachel remembered that when Mrs. Talansky died, her mother had cooked meals for Sacha and his father for weeks, and had even mended their clothes, until Mr. Talansky was able to cope on his own. And when Mr. Gervitz's wife was ill, Rachel's mother had gone over every afternoon to make tea and read to her. Now, when Mrs. Berlatsky was clearly in need of a friend, Rachel's mother seemed incapable of knowing what to say or do; it was as if she was suddenly devoid of empathy.

Leaving the Berlatskys in search of a wagon to take Chaia to the hospital, Rachel led her mother and Nucia toward another wooden outdoor shed. At one time it had been painted red, but most of the color had peeled off or faded. As they walked past, Rachel saw that the wooden door was broken and scattered across the ground. She let go of Nucia's hand, examined the dim opening, and saw a foot clad in a familiar black felt boot. Rachel's stomach lurched, and chills ran up and down her body as her eyes made their way from the foot to the head. It was her father, his body contorted and covered in blood. She fell backwards, her head spinning until everything went dark.

Three

Sergei barged through the heavy oak doors of the police station, past a group of officers huddled together smoking and speaking in solemn voices, to his father's office in the back corner. He yanked the door open and saw his father sitting at his desk, facing three men—Petya's father, Mayor Schmidt, who had copper-red hair like Petya, Governor von Raben, and another burly man Sergei didn't know, in a military uniform with a red vest and gold epaulets.

"You did nothing to stop the riots; you watched as innocent people were attacked!" Sergei's voice rose with every word. "And I even heard that you insulted Jews while they were being beaten." He paused, expecting his father to jump out of his seat and hit him across his face.

"How dare you barge in here like this," roared Sergei's father, his eyes darting between his son and the three men in front of him.

"If you had only believed me," Sergei continued. "If you had questioned Mikhail's uncle and cousin, you would have seen that they needed Mikhail out of the way, and this whole riot would have been avoided." Sergei moved closer until he was at his father's desk. "Children wouldn't be orphans today if this pogrom hadn't taken place; if the murderer had been found, none of this would have happened." Sergei stared defiantly at his father and saw that his eyes were bloodshot; his pupils were blazing.

"Is this true, Aleksandr?" asked Mayor Schmidt. "Is Sergei speaking the truth?"

Sergei's father's face grew red and beads of sweat dripped from his hairline. "The boy told me that somebody had witnessed the murder, but I didn't think there was any truth to it." He glared at Sergei with contempt.

"Your job is to take any information you receive seriously," said Governor von Raben, leaning over the desk. "I can assure you that we will look into this matter thoroughly."

"And I can assure you that I acted responsibly," Sergei's father replied.

"So that's it, Papa?" said Sergei, clenching his fists and feeling every muscle in his body tighten. "You won't even admit you were wrong?" He kicked his father's desk. "Even if I end up working in a factory, or peddling food in the market, I'll be more proud of myself than if I were police chief or the Imperial Police Director, because I'll be doing honest work, and I won't be hurting anybody."

Sergei turned and stomped out of his father's office.

"Wait a minute, Sergei," called Governor von Raben. "Come back in here."

Sergei stopped; his heart was racing. He took a couple of deep breaths, and returned to his father's office.

"Tell us everything you know," instructed the Governor.

"Mikhail's uncle and cousin killed him."

"You have no proof of this," said Sergei's father. He threw Sergei a dismissive look.

"Let us hear what the boy has to say," said Governor von Raben. "How did you get this information in the first place, Sergei?"

"I have a friend who saw the whole thing."

"Why didn't this friend come forward himself?" said Mayor Schmidt.

"Because my friend is Jewish, and a girl," he answered, aware that his father would be shocked by the fact that the witness was not only Jewish, but female as well.

"Well of course she didn't come forward," said the man in the military uniform. "She was trying to throw people off the Jewish scent."

"That's not true," said Sergei. "She's terrified that Mikhail's uncle will come after her if she says anything. I've promised not to reveal her name."

"Mikhail's uncle, Vasily Rybachenko, is a former police officer," Sergei's father continued, cutting off Sergei.

"That's not possible," interrupted Mayor Schmidt. "A police officer would never stab a boy to death."

"Aleksandr, what do you know about this officer Rybachenko?" asked von Raben.

Sergei's father rubbed his whiskers before answering. "He was dismissed for threatening a fellow officer."

"When?" demanded Mayor Schmidt. Sergei's father

shuffled some papers around on his desk, pulled one from the pile, and squinted at it. "The seventh of February."

"Two days before Mikhail was killed," said Sergei slowly. "His uncle probably wanted to inherit the family's tobacco plant; Mikhail was supposed to take over for his grandfather one day."

The room grew silent. All eyes were on Sergei's father.

"I remember Mikhail telling me that his uncle had a gambling problem," Sergei continued. "So Mikhail's grandfather was going to leave everything to Mikhail."

"Surely the old man would leave Vasily something." Governor von Raben twirled his mustache with his thumb and forefinger.

Sergei shook his head. "Mikhail's grandfather had cut Vasily off years ago, and with Mikhail's parents gone, everything was going to go to Mikhail."

"What about the cousin?" asked Mayor Schmidt.

"Philip," said Sergei. "My friend heard Mikhail begging Philip to help him that day."

"How long have you had this information about Vasily and his son, Aleksandr?" asked Mayor Schmidt.

Sergei's father closed his eyes for a moment before answering. "A couple of weeks."

"We could have arrested Vasily and Philip, announced that the police had solved this murder, and put an end to the idea of a pogrom," said Governor von Raben. Sergei's father hung his head. "I know. I put my prejudices ahead of justice, ahead of my own son. I will carry that shame for the rest of my years."

Sergei saw remorse in his father's eyes, but then he recalled Mikhail's blood on the river, Menahem's small, tear-stained face, and the lifeless faces of the dead being carted off like animals, and he wasn't sure he'd ever be able to forgive the defeated man who stood before him.

❄❄❄

Rachel watched Chaia being loaded onto a horse-drawn wagon. Chaia's long blonde hair, streaked with dirt and blood, draped over the sides of the board that held her motionless body. The rest of the Berlatskys climbed onto the wagon and with a jolt were off to the hospital, along with hundreds of others with no place else to go.

Rachel clutched Snegurochka's wooden head as she followed the wagon with her mother and sister. The clip-clop of the horse's hooves was a comforting, familiar sound, the only normal part of the day. As they walked, they were joined by more people, all carrying their treasured belongings, their faces pale and despondent. Rachel reached into her blue muslin pouch, touched the six chess pieces, and then the pages from her journal. They were all she'd been able to salvage from her home, all she had to remind her of her father and her life before the riots.

When she saw the crowd gathered at the Jewish Hospital, Rachel fought back tears. Being forced to take refuge in this large, imposing building made everything more real and painful. Lining up to get a place to sleep was almost too much to bear, and yet, there was no other choice.

A tall, plain woman greeted them at the gate to the hospital's courtyard. "I'm the matron," she explained to Rachel's mother. "Can I have your name and the number of people in your family?"

Rachel waited for her mother or Nucia to speak, but they stared at the woman blankly, as if they hadn't understood the question.

"Rachel Paskar and we have four...I mean..." She gulped and paused. "Three people in our family: my mother, Ita, my sister, Nucia, and me."

The woman carefully recorded their names in a notebook with a feather pen. "I must tell you that space is limited here now, and getting scarcer by the minute. To tell you the truth, we have at least four hundred people spread throughout the building, and just one hundred and ten beds, so I'm afraid there's not much privacy. But you'll be glad to hear we are separating men and women—men on the first floor, women and children on the second."

Rachel nodded.

"I'm also not sure how long you can stay; we don't really know what lies ahead, do we?"

Rachel shook her head.

"Now, are any of you injured in any way?" Her voice was smooth and efficient, as if she had repeated the same words over and over.

"No," said Rachel. She watched the woman's eyes scour her body for blood, bumps, and bruises.

"Fine." The woman made a note on her paper.

"The Berlatskys...they arrived just before us," said Rachel. "Could we be in a room with them?"

"Well, let me see." The woman looked over her notes and frowned. "Yes, one girl was badly injured. She's in a treatment room. You can stay with the rest of the family in the ward." She gestured to the area behind her. "Walk through the courtyard and once inside, take the stairs on your right to the second floor. Follow the corridor until it ends and turn left. It's room 28, on your left."

"Thank you," mumbled Rachel.

"My name is Rena, if you have any questions or problems."

Rachel turned back to thank Rena again, but she was already talking to another group of new arrivals.

The courtyard was a stark square surrounded by dirty white cement walls. It looked shabby and old. As her eyes moved around the dingy area, Rachel saw something in the far corner. Squinting to see better, she cried out "Ei!" when she saw dead bodies stacked neatly against the wall like birch logs. Is this where they would bring her father? To be callously piled as if he was worth no more than firewood?

"Are you all right, Rachel?" asked Nucia.

Feeling as if she might vomit, Rachel waited a minute before she was able to respond. "Don't look around," she said in a dry voice. "Keep your eyes straight ahead."

Inside, the air was stale and smelled like sweat, soap, and urine. Men sat in the dimly lit corridor, their backs against the wall, with the same vacant expression Rachel saw on her mother. She wondered if her own face looked that empty.

As they walked past room after room, she gasped. So many men were crammed into the small spaces, lying on cots and the bare floor, talking and groaning.

"Look, there's Mr. Gervitz!" Nucia exclaimed, pointing to an elderly man asleep in the hall.

"It's not fair," Rachel whispered. Why had he survived instead of her father? Her tears were unstoppable as she trudged through the building.

Rachel climbed the stairs slowly, her legs heavy, as if they were bags of potatoes. She took a deep breath and then entered the stuffy room. There were ten narrow metal cots with their heads to the wall, five on each side of the room. The space between the beds was no more than the length of her father's violin, and the passageway down the middle was only wide enough for two people side by side. One old woman rocked back and forth with her eyes closed as she sat on a cot. She didn't appear to be hurt, but her clothing was splattered with blood.

"Rachel, is that you?" Esther Berlatsky appeared from the shadows in the corner. She stood in front of the last cot on the right-hand side of the room. Huddled behind her were Mrs. Berlatsky, Elena, and Jacob.

Rachel rushed over to them and found herself in a comforting embrace. "How is Chaia?"

Mrs. Berlatsky dabbed her eyes with a handkerchief. "The doctor didn't have time to speak to me when we arrived. So many people. She was taken away without a word." Mrs. Berlatsky's eyes rested on Rachel for a second before welling up with tears. Jacob, his face gray and wan, flung his arms around his mother and started crying as well.

Rachel stepped back as Elena and Esther tried to console their mother, embarrassed to witness their private sorrow. She turned her head and saw her mother climb onto the empty cot beside the Berlatskys. Without uttering a single word, her mother closed her eyes and turned onto her side, her back facing Rachel.

While Nucia embraced the Berlatskys, Rachel looked around and realized that there were no more empty beds. A few children slept fitfully on the floor and a number of beds held two women. One small square window overlooked the courtyard, but Rachel turned away from it. She didn't want to see the stacks of bodies again.

❄❄❄

It was difficult to sleep on the hard floor, wedged in between her sister and Esther Berlatsky. A thin, brown cotton cover was folded over them, but Rachel pushed it down. It smelled strange and musty, reminding her of all that had happened even when she closed her eyes and tried to pretend that nothing had changed...that she was safe at home with her parents and sister...that tomorrow would be another normal day.

But tomorrow would be far from normal. Life would never be the same or as good without her father. Rachel recalled his last words, how he had promised her that he would make sure everyone in the house was safe, and then join them in the outhouse. If only he had come with them right away, she thought. He would be in the hospital with them right now. She would have his strong shoulders to lean on, his infinite wisdom to guide her through the difficult days ahead.

Rachel tossed and turned, groaned, and sat up. A soft light from the moon streamed in through the window just like it had at her house, reminding Rachel that the outside world was unchanged, unaffected by these riots. For people far away in Petersburg and Moscow, life would go on as usual. And the *Bessarabetz,* filled with the lies that had led to these attacks, would continue to be published without penalty. It all seemed bitterly unfair.

Nucia sat up beside Rachel.

"What are we going to do?" whispered Rachel.

"I don't know," said Nucia quietly.

"Where are we going to live? Our house is gone. And how are we going to pay for food?"

"Shh! You'll get Mother upset." Nucia squinted at Rachel and yawned. "Why don't you go back to sleep?"

"I can't. Every time I close my eyes, I think of Father."

"You must try. We need to be strong for Mother." Nucia sighed and lay back down. Rachel listened to the noises in the room. Across from her, someone snored loudly. A few babies were crying, and many of the women wept softly. Rachel couldn't cry anymore. Every tear she had in her had been shed for her father. A hollowness had settled inside of her, a hole that could never be filled.

"No…no…no! My children…don't hurt them…no…No!"

Rachel turned in the direction of the voice and saw a woman in the hallway yelling at a nurse. The woman's long hair hung wildly around her face.

"Please calm down. You're in a hospital," said the nurse. "I'm trying to help you."

"Where are my children?"

"They're gone."

"No, they can't be dead. They're only children. They've done no harm. You're lying. Tell me…where are they?"

The woman's desperate screams woke everyone in the room. All eyes were on her as she called for her children. Eventually, a couple of orderlies carried her away, but her voice could still be heard as she was taken down the corridor, and it echoed in Rachel's head until dawn.

❄❄❄

Funerals could not be held inside the synagogue because it was an ashen shell, destroyed in the riots. Rachel couldn't believe how the building had been burned into charred remains. Worst of all were the desecrated Torah scrolls. Scattered all over the ground, the sacred scrolls were black at the edges and burned completely through in parts. Rachel wondered if this was a sign that Jews should abandon their traditions, go forward believing only in what they could see, feel, taste, and hear—birch trees that provided welcome shade in the summer, rain that made fruit and vegetables grow, the sweet smell of lavender in the spring, fish that kept bellies full in the winter, brisk wind that howled in the night, and violin music that warmed hearts and souls. What purpose did faith have? How had it improved their lives?

"This is horrible," said Sacha. His curls were barely evident, flattened by dirt and grease, and his eyes were outlined in dark shadows. He and his father were also staying at the hospital because their home had been destroyed. "I can't believe the scrolls weren't burned entirely to ashes."

Rachel looked away and tried to swallow the lump in her throat. She wondered if her father's faith would be shaken right now, like hers, if he would be devastated by this sight, or more committed to their faith than ever before.

The rabbi said a prayer asking for peace for all of the forty-nine victims. It was early afternoon, two days after the massacre, and Rachel stood facing the dead who lay on the ground at the Jewish cemetery. Since there were not enough coffins, the bodies were wrapped in prayer shawls.

Rachel listened to Rabbi Yitzchak with an impassive face, and her hands shook as she tore her clothing at the gravesite to honor her father. She didn't know what to believe anymore… was being Jewish worth all the pain and suffering her family had endured? While everyone else said the *Kaddish* to mark the end of the burial service, Rachel closed her eyes and listened to the words of the prayer.

"May His illustrious name be blessed always and forever… Blessed, praised, glorified, exalted, extolled, honored, raised up, and acclaimed to be the name of the Holy One, blessed be He, beyond every blessing, hymn, praise and consolation that is uttered in the world. And let us say Amen. May abundant peace from heaven and life be upon us and upon all Israel. And let us say Amen."

Rachel opened her eyes. The meaning of this prayer, which seemed strange given the occasion, confused her. The prayer didn't mention the dead, and she didn't understand why there was so much praise when so many were killed because they were Jewish. And as for peace, how could anyone expect peace when they were surrounded by such open hostility?

Warm tears started to flow down Rachel's cheeks. Sobs rose from her throat to her mouth. She hung her head down as her mother and sister threw clumps of earth over her father's shrouded body. Suddenly, she pictured her father in the ground, scratching at the earth to get out. "Father, Father!" she cried. "Don't put him in the dirt. He's not dead. Please, take him out of there. It's cold and dark underground. He doesn't belong there. Let him out! Please! Let him out!"

Strong arms pulled Rachel away from the grave. She struggled to break free, but the arms were stronger than she was.

"It's all right. Calm down. You'll be all right." Mr. Talansky held Rachel until her energy subsided and she wilted in his arms. She was hot and feverish, tired and empty, worn out with grief. Mr. Talansky picked Rachel up and carried her away from her father's grave.

"Where are we going?" Rachel looked at Mr. Talansky as he carried her.

"Back to the hospital," he said.

"I don't want to go back there. I want to go home." Rachel began crying, her tears falling onto Mr. Talansky's collar. Up ahead, through her blurry eyes, she saw Sacha, Nucia, and her mother. "We don't have Father anymore. What are we going to do?" Rachel lowered her eyes to see Mr. Talansky's face. The twinkle in his eyes was gone, replaced by despair.

"Here we are." He put Rachel down in front of the door to the hospital.

"You didn't answer my question," she said.

His eyes met hers. "That's because I do not have an answer."

❄❄❄

"She has three broken ribs, a broken leg, and a nasty cut on her head," said Mrs. Berlatsky to Rachel. They were standing beside Chaia's bed in the hospital, where she shared a room with a dozen other injured people. "Her body is going to mend but…" She looked at Rachel sadly. "She says nothing. Nothing."

Rachel gazed down at her friend who was barely recognizable with all the bandages. Her beautiful blonde hair had been cut and her head was covered in gauze. And her empty, glassy eyes stared up at the ceiling.

"Chaia…it's me, Rachel." She waited to see if her friend's

eyes moved or even blinked. Nothing. "Chaia…please look at me." Rachel glanced at Chaia's mother who nodded for her to continue. "I—" Rachel realized she didn't know what to say. There was no good news, nothing light to speak of. "I really miss you Chaia. You must wake up and see how awful I look because my hair hasn't been washed or brushed or braided in days and I've been wearing the same clothes, but I don't really mind because I know that soon we'll be able to go home and… and you'll get that bonnet you love so much…I just know it."

Rachel started to sob into her hands. She felt Mrs. Berlatsky's gentle touch around her shoulders as she led her away.

"You did very well, Rachel," said Mrs. Berlatsky. "I'm sure it will just take time until Chaia is with us again. Come. We must go and see how your mother is doing."

"She's not much better than Chaia," said Rachel. "No broken bones, but she doesn't speak. It's as if there is nothing inside of her."

"It has been a terrible time for all of us."

They walked down the corridor where moans drifted from doorways like a brisk fall wind.

"But why are you able to be so strong and my mother… why is she so weak?"

"Do not call your mother weak, Rachel," said Mrs. Berlatsky sternly. "She is one of the strongest people I've ever known."

"Then why—"

"Your mother is used to being in control, to planning and having things turn out the way she expects. This violence… losing your father…she needs time, like Chaia. She will come around. You will see." She squeezed Rachel's shoulders, which reassured her and made her feel hopeful.

❄❄❄

Rachel turned away with tears in her eyes as the doctor pulled the bloodstained blanket over the young woman's yellowish-gray face. For two days, the woman had been groaning in agony, though there were no visible signs of trauma. She had been louder than anyone else in their room, yet Rachel had become used to the sound. Now she was dead, and it was almost too quiet.

"Rachel, do you want to go for a walk?"

She looked up to see Sacha standing at the door to the room. He looked thin, gaunt, and tired. Rachel glanced at her mother who lay motionless on her cot, her eyes looking up at the white ceiling, and nodded. When she stood, a hunger pang ripped through her insides, and she had to balance herself on the wall until it went away. She tiptoed carefully over the people on the floor. Some slept, others were weeping, and a few talked quietly.

In the courtyard, Rachel inhaled the cool air. "Oh! I didn't realize how stifling it was in there."

"I know," said Sacha. "I hate being surrounded by strangers...all the time, every minute. There's nowhere to be alone."

As soon as they stepped outside the courtyard, Rachel gasped and clutched Sacha's arm. Though the bodies were gone, the road was still strewn with debris and she could see blood stains a few inches from her feet. Furniture had been pushed to the sides to make way for carriages, and there was an endless trail of broken glass, tiles, pieces of wood, and feathers. The air was thick with the scent of urine and lamp oil.

She let go of Sacha's arm, leaned on the courtyard wall, and began breathing heavily and with difficulty.

"I can't...I can't do this," she said. "I'm just not ready."

"That's all right." Sacha took her hand firmly and led her back into the courtyard.

"Do you think most gentiles want to hurt us?" she asked him when they were back inside the safety of the walls.

"No." He hesitated. "My father and I wouldn't be here without the help of a gentile family."

"What do you mean?" She pulled her hand from his, which was clammy and warm, and saw a pained expression flicker across his face.

"When the riots began on our street, we fled from our flat. At first, we ran along the street, ahead of the rioters, but they were catching up to us. Then a door opened—a red door—and a man with a kind face told us to come in for protection. Other Jews were already inside. We hid there for hours. The man and his wife fed us and made sure we were safe."

"I'm glad they took you in." His story reminded her of Sergei and how he had risked his own life to try and stop the rioters in her courtyard. He believed in her so completely, He didn't see her as a Jew but as a person equal to himself.

Rachel had a sudden urge to see Sergei, to thank him once more, and to get to know him better, but at the same time, she realized they would both be better off if their paths never crossed again.

Four

"What do you want?" The shopkeeper leaned over the counter. His fingers were stained yellow at the tips and the few teeth he had in his mouth were crooked and brown.

"Some tobacco please." Sergei looked down as he spoke to avoid the shopkeeper's foul breath. He hated buying anything from this disagreeable man, but he had the cheapest tobacco in Kishinev. The small store had shelves of cigarette papers, loose tobacco, pipes and cigars. A bold red advertisement for cigarettes hung on the wall, with a caricature of two well-dressed men sporting shiny white teeth. Outside, a policeman's voice rose above the crowd, ordering people to stay back on the sidewalk.

"A mess out there, yes?" muttered the shopkeeper. "They're waiting for Lopukhin to arrive."

"Who's he?" Petya asked.

"Head of the Imperial Police. Come to investigate the riots." He paused and leaned over the counter. "If you ask me, the Yids brought all this on themselves."

"What are you talking about?" Sergei clenched his fists to keep his temper from getting the better of him.

"The newspaper says they've been taking over Kishinev. Putting us out of business. Time we did something about it." He stopped speaking for a moment to wipe his brow with a dirty cloth. "Twenty kopecks."

"Even if they do put people out of business, it's not illegal, and it's not worth killing for," Sergei said, glaring at the shopkeeper. He threw the kopecks on the counter and headed to the door.

"You have to stop arguing with people," Petya said to Sergei as soon as they were outside. "You're going—"

A sharp jingling sound interrupted Petya as they stepped onto the crowded sidewalk. The boys looked to their left and watched a large closed carriage coming along the street, led by two majestic horses adorned with necklets, bells, and foxtails. When it came closer, Sergei could see from the intricate carvings on the carriage that it carried someone important.

Unable to get away from the mob of people, the boys watched as the carriage passed by. The passenger, a middle-aged man with gray hair and black, turned-up whiskers, wore round spectacles and stared straight ahead, ignoring the hordes of people gaping at him.

"Come on," said Sergei. He slipped in front of the crowd and onto the street.

"That must be the police official the shopkeeper talked about," said Petya.

Sergei nodded, his eyes pasted on the Jewish people lining the road. They were disheveled, with torn clothing, and many had open wounds. Turning a corner, Sergei and Petya left the crowd behind them. "Is he going to see your father?" Petya asked.

"I don't know. I haven't spoken with my father much. He's been in a pretty bad mood since the riots."

"How come? It's not like they were his fault."

"I saw a telegraph he received last night. The military troops are staying here for a while to make sure nobody else gets hurt. I don't think my father likes having people watching over him."

"Well, at least your father didn't hide when all the fighting was going on. My father could at least have pretended to do something." Petya shook his head and scowled.

"I don't know. My father paraded around, watched the attacks, and did absolutely nothing." Sergei turned to leave. "I'll see you later."

"Where are you going?" asked Petya.

Sergei wanted to tell Petya about Rachel, and how worried he was about her, but he knew this would be a mistake. "To find someone."

❄❄❄

In the hospital's courtyard. Sergei stared, open-mouthed, at the patients sitting mutely on the steps, heads and arms wrapped in bandages, pain etched on their faces. Weeping—anguished cries—accosted him when he opened the door. The sharp, overpowering smell of antiseptic mixed with the putrid odor of perspiration filled his nose and mouth. He watched in disbelief as a crippled man, whose eye had been gouged out, begged a nurse to kill him. He saw men talking to themselves, their bodies covered in sores, bumps, and bruises. He saw a young girl sitting alone, her arms around her knees as she rocked back and forth. Her eyes were empty of life.

A sea of people sat hunched over in the waiting room, their ragged clothing torn and bloody, their faces lined in sorrow. Sergei pressed his hands to his eyes, unable to witness any more despair; just then, someone grabbed the back of his legs. Startled, he turned around and saw Menahem. He picked the boy up and gave him a big hug. When he tried to put him down, Menahem wouldn't let go.

"How are they treating you? Are you getting enough to eat?" Sergei could feel Menahem's bony spine through his shirt.

Menahem nodded. "We go to the soup kitchen every day, and they give us bread too."

"You and your grandmother?"

"No…she…she's gone." Menahem's lower lip began to tremble.

Sergei could tell the boy was trying to be brave. "Who's taking care of you?"

"Some of the nurses."

"I wish I could help you," said Sergei.

"Can I come home with you?" Menahem asked. "I'll be good. I promise."

Sergei's eyes watered as he hugged Menahem tighter. He wished he could hold onto Menahem's innocence and trust forever, and that Menahem would never see him as the enemy. "I can't take you, but I promise I'll visit you as much as I can."

Menahem's body went limp in Sergei's arms, and he sunk his head onto Sergei's shoulder. "I won't be here much longer. I have to go to the orphanage soon."

Frustrated by this news, Sergei was trying to think of something positive to say, when he saw Rachel walking toward him. Relief swelled inside his chest as she drew closer and he saw that she was physically unharmed.

"Sergei—" she said, her face breaking into a smile. Dark circles underlined her red eyes and her untidy hair hung in her face. "Who is he?" She glanced curiously at Menahem and then at Sergei.

"My friend, Menahem. Menahem, this is Rachel."

Menahem lifted his head and looked shyly at Rachel. "He brought me here when my grandmother…" Tears streamed down Menahem's face. He buried his head in Sergei's shoulder again.

"I was here, the day of the…you weren't…I went to your house but I couldn't find anybody," Sergei said.

"I was hiding in the outhouse; I heard you asking people to stop." She swallowed and took a deep breath. "That was very brave of you."

Sergei hung his head, disturbed by the thought of Rachel hiding in a smelly outhouse. "I wish they had listened."

"My father was killed, and Chaia's father," said Rachel in a flat voice. "Chaia has many broken bones and doesn't speak. She saw her father…" Her voice broke and she turned away from Sergei.

"I know it doesn't bring anyone back, but many people have been arrested," he said slowly, watching her reaction. "And Mikhail's uncle and cousin are being investigated. My father finally revealed what I told him."

Rachel sniffed and wiped her tears. "I guess that's good news. Still, I've lost everything because of horrible lies. We don't know where we'll be in a month from now, or even a week."

"Are you going to have to go to the orphanage, too?" Menahem said to Rachel.

She shook her head. "I don't think so."

Sergei looked past her at the people sprawled all over the floor. He shifted Menahem's weight to his other shoulder. "I want to help you."

"How?"

"With money, finding a place for you to live…"

"You don't work…and you don't owe us anything." She looked back down the shadowy corridor. "I have to go now. My mother needs me."

Sergei's eyes followed her as she walked away. "Damm!" Rage built up inside of him like a fire fed with oil. He kicked the wall. "Dammit!"

A few patients sitting in the corridor cowered during Sergei's outburst.

"Are you mad at me?" asked Menahem in a meek voice.

Sergei winced, embarrassed that he'd frightened Menahem with his display of anger. He crouched over and put Menahem on the floor. "No, of course I'm not mad at you. I didn't mean to—" He bit his lip and tried to figure out the best words to say. "I'm mad at the people who hurt your grandmother and Rachel's father." He hung his head. "I want to make things right, but nothing I do will ever be enough."

He felt a warm hand take his as he looked into Menahem's hopeful eyes.

"You helped me," said Menahem. "That was good."

Sergei smiled and tousled his hair. "I guess that was good. Now I just need to do something good for Rachel."

❄❄❄

Rachel wiggled her toes to keep them from falling asleep. She'd been standing in the soup-kitchen line for almost two hours and was still a long way from the front. Just ahead of them were Elena and Esther Berlatsky with their arms around Jacob. Mrs. Berlatsky and Rachel's mother stood silently in front of Rachel.

"At least Mother came with us today," said Rachel to Nucia.

"Yes. This will be the first time she's eaten since…"

"I know."

The girls stood quietly for a few minutes as the line moved slowly forward.

"I want to sit down," Rachel told Nucia. "My shoes are so tight I can hardly feel my feet."

Nucia shook her head. "The ground is dirty and wet. Stay standing."

Rachel sighed but did as her sister said. Since they'd arrived at the hospital, Nucia had taken on the authoritative role in their family. Much to her surprise, Rachel didn't mind at all. She liked having someone watching over her the way her father had.

They shuffled forward, a bit closer to the food, only to stop again. "What if they run out of soup?" asked Rachel.

"Then we don't eat," said Nucia. "But they've had enough every day so far."

Rachel turned to see how far the line went behind them. Familiar faces surfaced as she scanned the swarm of people. Anna, a girl she knew from school…Yoram, with his pensive eyes and straight black hair…and Leah, her head bandaged where her hair used to be.

"Leah!" she called, rushing back to greet her.

The color drained from Rachel's cheeks when she saw her friend's face. Leah's skin was bruised, in varying shades of purple and gray, and a raw-looking gash ran diagonally from her ear to her nose. She opened her arms and pulled Rachel into a tight embrace.

"Oh Rachel," said Leah, loosening her hold. "I'm so glad to see you're all right."

Rachel looked down at her feet, riddled with shame for making it through the riots without a blemish while her two closest friends would be scarred for life. She lifted her head and gazed at Leah. "What about you? What happened?"

"Well..." Leah lowered her eyes. "A few fists and a knife ran into my face and head during the riots...I'm doing better now, but my parents are still unable to leave the hospital because of their injuries."

"Your head...does it hurt?" asked Rachel.

"Not as much as it did." She took a deep breath. "The worst was when they had to shave my hair off."

"I'm so sorry, Leah."

Tears welled up in Leah's eyes. "Meyer is in bad shape, completely blinded during the attacks."

"Oh no," cried Rachel. She knew how much Leah cared for Meyer and feared this would affect or even ruin their future together.

Through her tears, Leah asked about Chaia. Rachel saw Yoram twist his head sharply to hear her reply. When Rachel explained briefly what had happened, Yoram grew pale. Leah averted her eyes for a moment before speaking. "That night... the things I saw...what those men did to me..."

Rachel gasped.

"I can never talk about what happened ever again."

"I'll never ask you to tell me," said Rachel. "I'm just grateful you're here." She glanced ahead and saw that her mother and sister were near the front of the line. After planning to meet in the courtyard the next day, she left Leah and rejoined her family. She looked back to make sure Leah was still there, and that she hadn't imagined their conversation. Leah was still in the same place, but Yoram was gone.

❄❄❄

The soup tasted like hot water. There were tiny bits of cabbage that had floated to the bottom, but the broth was tasteless. And the tiny piece of bread she'd been given was hard to swallow because it was so dry.

When she placed her empty bowl in a wooden bucket piled high with other dirty bowls, she saw Sacha and his father hovering nearby. Both of them looked like skeletons of their former selves, their faces drawn so that their bones stuck out. Mr. Talansky's hand shook when he placed his bowl in the bucket.

"We were among the first in line," said Sacha to Rachel. "But it wasn't enough to fill a bird."

"I know. And I couldn't taste any cabbage in my soup." Rachel noticed Sacha's eyes darting back and forth from her face to the bucket filled with discarded bowls. Turning her head, she saw Mr. Talansky grabbing bowls and holding them up to his mouth, licking the remains of other people's soup.

"We're both so hungry. What they give us isn't enough." Sacha fidgeted with his hands and looked down in shame. "I'm sorry you had to see that."

"Don't be. I'm still hungry, and I'm not nearly as big as you or your father. It's all right," she said, disconcerted by Mr. Talansky's desperate condition. "As soon as I finished my bowl, I started counting the hours until the next meal."

Sacha kicked at the ground. "We're leaving tomorrow."

"Where are you going?"

"Petersburg. My father has a sister there. We're going to stay with her family until my father gets a job."

Rachel twisted her braid and forced a smile. Sacha and his father had been like family to her, and now they were leaving. She might never see them again.

"Maybe your family could come too," Sacha continued, his voice becoming earnest. "Maybe your mother could get a position..." His voice tapered off as he spoke, as if he knew what she was going to say.

"Doing what? All my mother knows how to do is cook and clean."

"Well...she could get a job at a restaurant...or doing needlework."

Rachel glanced at her mother who stood waiting for Mrs. Berlatsky to finish her soup. She was stooped over, as if she were sixty, not thirty-three. Her hair was streaked with gray and her face was pale, almost translucent.

"I don't think so," Rachel said. "My mother's hardly spoken in days. All she does is sleep. I can't see her making food or even doing needlework. Not for a long time; maybe never."

"Then...maybe *you* could come with us," said Sacha.

Rachel felt his eyes on her. "I can't leave my mother or sister. It wouldn't be right." She looked up at him sadly. "But

I will miss you and your father." She glanced at Mr. Talansky, now sitting on the wet ground. "Will you promise to write me?"

Sacha nodded and gave her a rueful smile. She watched as he helped his father to his feet and headed back to the hospital. The Talanskys were another link to her former life that was now being broken. Little by little, her life was disintegrating, leaving her feeling helpless and despondent about the future.

❄❄❄

Rachel and Nucia stood in the doorway to their hospital room staring at their mother. She lay motionless on her cot.

"I'm so worried about her," said Nucia. "She's lost so much weight and has no energy at all."

"She hardly ate anything yesterday," said Rachel. "And at night she's restless, rolling around and groaning."

"I wish we could take her away from here. Sacha and his father are lucky they have family in Petersburg."

Rachel pushed her braids behind her shoulders. "We do have family…Father's parents. Bubbe and Zeyde."

"We've never even met his parents," sighed Nucia.

A smile extended across Rachel's face. "Let's write them a letter. We'll tell them what happened and ask if we can come."

Nucia looked at Rachel as if she was crazy. "They might ignore a letter. They don't know us at all…we don't even know where they live."

Rachel fixed her gaze on Nucia. "I know the town. We can address it to the synagogue there. We have to try. That's what Father would say. When they hear about Father…" her voice broke, and she paused to gain her composure. "They may want to help us."

Nucia shrugged her shoulders. "I think you're wasting your time."

Rachel's eyes flashed with hope and determination. "All we have right now is time. There is nothing to lose." She turned and strode purposefully down the hall to Rena's office.

Rena sat at her tidy desk filling out some forms. "Rena? Is there an inkwell and pen I can use to write a letter?" asked Rachel.

"Yes, of course. Use mine." Rena gestured to her pewter inkwell. "And here's a piece of paper."

Rachel sat down on the chair facing Rena, laid the paper flat on the desk, and dipped the quill into the ink.

Zeyde and Bubbe, Sholom aleichem, she wrote neatly at the top of the page. *We hope you are well. We are sorry to bring you bad news.* Rachel paused to take a deep breath. When she continued, her hand shook, causing drops of ink to pool on the paper. *Father was killed during a big fight that took place in Kishinev at the end of Passover. Our house was destroyed. Now we're staying in the hospital but have to find a new place to live.*

Rachel read over what she had written but was unsure of how to continue. "Rena...do you think it's a good idea to write my grandparents and ask if we can live with them, when we've never even met them?"

Rena set her pen in its stand and sat back with a thoughtful look on her face. "I think it's an excellent idea. I'm sure your grandparents have wanted to meet you for a long time..."

"You don't understand," said Rachel. "My father had a quarrel with his parents years ago, and they never saw each other again."

Rena leaned forward and rested her elbows on the desk. "I

don't know your grandparents, but I am quite sure they deeply regret the argument that came between them and your father. Because of it, they don't know you and your sister, and worse, their son has died before they could resolve their differences." She looked intently at Rachel. "They won't want the same thing to happen again."

Rachel nodded, encouraged by Rena's sensible words. With renewed determination, she continued writing. *Mother has hardly spoken since the massacre. She won't be able to work for some time. We would be very grateful if we could come and stay with you until Mother feels better. We promise we won't cause any trouble, and we have always wanted to meet you both very much. Please send your reply to the Kishinev Jewish Hospital. Your loving granddaughter, Rachel.*

She finished writing and set the pen in the inkwell. "I don't have a stamp. How am I going to get it to them?"

"Don't worry," said Rena. "Since the riot, the hospital has been receiving donations to help pay for food, clothing, and medical care. I'll get the money from this fund."

Rachel stared at the envelope addressed to her grandparents, then handed it carefully to Rena. "This is our only hope. The only family we have."

❄❄❄

"What the devil! This is rubbish...absolute rubbish." Sergei's father stared at the document in his hands. "I did what I could with the men I had."

Sergei looked up from the game of backgammon he was playing with Natalya. His father had just received a telegraph from his office and had been shouting at it for the last five minutes.

"It's your turn, Sergei." Natalya prodded him to pay attention.

"Oh no! You put me on the bar. Now I have to start all over again." Sergei pretended to be upset that his sister was making him start from the beginning.

Natalya grinned. "I'm going to beat you! I'm going to win!"

He smiled wanly, envious of his sister's youth, of her inability to fully understand the gravity of the situation in Kishinev.

Sergei's father ripped the telegraph message into pieces and threw them on the floor. Since his admission to the mayor and the governor, Sergei had seen his father fly into a rage every day, as he received such documents from his superiors.

"What's wrong, Aleksandr?" Sergei's mother turned from the dishes she'd been washing.

His father began pacing. "They're all idiots! Idiots, I tell you! Saying I didn't do my job…I'd like to see them do better. There were thousands of rioters. What could I do?" He waved his arm in the air as he raged. "Besides, Mikhail's uncle and cousin were arrested at their home last night. There will be a trial. Justice will be done. What more do they want?"

"I'm sure you did everything you could, Aleksandr." Sergei's mother tried to put her arms around him, but he pushed her away.

Sergei frowned; his mother had no idea that his father could have averted the riots entirely.

Carlotta sat by the stove, knitting a yellow shawl. She cleared her throat loudly. "You cannot pull a fish out of a pond without labor," she said.

"Be quiet!" Sergei's father barked at Carlotta. "If you want to keep a roof overhead and food in your belly, be quiet for heaven's sake!"

"Is someone mad at you, Papa?" asked Natalya.

Sergei's father stood still and stared at Natalya. "Sergei, take your sister outside. To the square. The merry-go-round should be working again. Take her there."

"But we haven't finished our game yet, Papa," cried Natalya. "And I'm going to beat Sergei!"

"Do as you're told, Natalya." Their mother looked at her and Sergei with an expression that left little room for argument.

Sergei stood up and faced his father. "You waited until after the riots to arrest Mikhail's uncle. You wanted to see the Jews ruined; and you don't really feel bad about not coming forward earlier, you're only upset because people blame you for what happened."

His father glared at him, his eyes boring into Sergei like knives. Sergei's knees started to buckle. Before he knew what was happening, his father slapped him across the face. "You're too mouthy for your own good! Get out of here before I hit you again. Harder."

"No! Papa, don't," cried Natalya. She ran to her mother who turned to face her husband.

"Aleksandr! Stop this right now."

Sergei ran to the door and bolted down the stairs. His face burned from his father's hand.

"Are you all right?" Natalya's voice startled him. Sergei had not realized she was behind him. Natalya peered anxiously at his face.

"Is there a red mark there?" he asked her, feeling the sore area with his hand.

"Yes, but I'm sure it will go away soon, Sergei." She paused. "What's wrong with Papa? He's been really mad lately."

They reached the ground floor and walked out to the street. "Well…when you do something wrong and people find out about it, you don't feel very good," he said.

"Like the time I took the new pink ribbon from Maria's doll for my doll, and put my old pink ribbon on hers?"

Sergei gave his sister a half smile. "I think Papa has more at stake than a ribbon, but yes, it's sort of the same thing."

"When will Papa be happy again?"

She looked so innocent that Sergei hoped she'd never find out what their father was really like. "I don't know."

"Will you promise not to make him so upset, Sergei? I don't like seeing him hit you."

"I'll try. I really will. But I can't promise. Sometimes he makes me so angry, I can't help it."

"I wish you'd promise," she said, putting her small hand in his.

Sergei looked at her upturned face. "I'll do my best."

❄❄❄

"You've got to believe me. I won't hurt Menahem. I just want to talk to him. He was moved from the hospital before I had a chance to see him," Sergei pleaded with a woman wearing a black kerchief on her head. Her expression was hard to gauge in the dim light.

"My father is the chief of police, remember? And you told

me yesterday that I'd be able to see Menahem today." Sergei tried to imitate his father's authoritative voice.

The woman put down her pen and regarded him for a moment. "You have to be eighteen in order to sign a child out from the orphanage."

"I am eighteen," Sergei lied. He would be fifteen in one month, so it wasn't a horrible lie.

She looked him up and down. "You don't look eighteen."

"You should see my father. He looks even younger than I do."

She gave him a skeptical look and sighed. "All right. You can take him for two hours. But first I need some information." She rifled through the papers on her desk and handed one to Sergei.

"Do you promise not to fill his head with dreams about the future?" She glanced at Sergei and began writing something. "His future is here. It's unlikely he'll leave the orphanage until he's sixteen, so promises of any kind would be devastating."

"What can I promise? Friendship. That's all I have to give him." Sergei finished writing down his name, address, phone number, and his fictional age.

"Wait here. I'll go and get the boy." She stood up and headed down a long, narrow hallway. The floorboards creaked with every step she took.

Sergei looked away from the stained walls as he waited. What if Menahem was mad at him for taking so long to visit? What if Menahem was upset that he couldn't help him get out of the orphanage?

"Sergei!" Menahem ran up to him and gave him a big hug. "I knew you'd come. I knew you wouldn't break your promise."

Sergei held him tightly. "You look good. A bit skinny but good," he told Menahem.

"The food tastes terrible here." Menahem made a face.

"Well then, how about I take you out for something to eat?" Sergei smiled at Menahem and tousled his hair.

"Let's go!" Menahem was already on his way to the heavy door.

❄❄❄

"How are your *pirozhki*?" Sergei watched Menahem finish the last pastry filled with mashed potatoes. They were eating in a small, rundown restaurant in the Jewish quarter, one of the few restaurants that had re-opened after the riots. Sergei had paid for the meal with money he'd been saving for train fare out of Kishinev.

"Good!" Menahem grinned. He had a dab of potato in the corner of his mouth.

"I'm not that hungry. You can finish mine if you want." Sergei pushed his plate over to Menahem.

"Really?"

"Listen, I'm sorry it's been so long since I've seen you. I meant to come earlier, but I've been looking for a job."

"That's all right. I'm just glad you came. You're my first visitor." Menahem polished off the pirozhki from Sergei's plate and looked up happily.

"I'll try to come a couple of times a week, after school," Sergei said.

"That will be good!"

"So...is it all right, living at the orphanage?" Sergei looked at Menahem and saw a flicker of pain cross the boy's face.

"I guess. Mostly we have to stay on our beds when we're not doing our chores. The lady in charge only yells if we get off our beds or if we don't do our chores the right way."

"What about school?"

"It was wrecked in the riots."

"Do you have any books to read?"

"No."

"Playing cards?"

"No."

"I'll try to bring some books with me the next time I come." Sergei didn't know what else to say.

"I don't know if you can bring me anything. We're not allowed to own things the other children don't have. That way there won't be any fights. This one boy had a wooden boat that his father had carved for him. But an older boy stole it and smashed it into pieces."

Sergei frowned. Menahem was small for his age, and too trusting. There was no way he would survive until his sixteenth birthday in the orphanage.

Five

"I need a few women and girls to sew garments," said Rena, walking into their room and opening the curtains. Rachel, who was curled up beside her mother, sat up and shaded her eyes to protect them from the sharp morning light. Some women and children were still sleeping; others were talking quietly. She was losing track of time with no school schedule to frame her day, and she was sleeping more and more to pass the long hours.

"What time is it?" she groaned.

"Ten thirty," said Rena. "You've already slept half the morning."

"Oh, I'm still tired." Rachel dropped back down beside her mother, who hadn't stirred.

Nucia's head appeared as she rolled out from under the cot where she had been sleeping. "Where are Elena and Esther?"

"Visiting Chaia," said Rena. She clapped her hands together and looked at Rachel's mother who had just opened her eyes. "Mrs. Paskar…I understand you and your daughters are talented seamstresses. The Society in Aid of the Poor Jews of Kishinev has raised money to make clothes for victims of the massacre. Two thousand families have been left with nothing after the riots. You would be paid for your efforts."

Rachel's mother faced Rena and blinked.

"I don't think my mother has the strength," said Rachel. "She's lost weight since we arrived at the hospital and hardly eats anything at the soup kitchen."

Rena put her hands on her hips and stared at Rachel's mother. "Nonsense. I think your mother needs to be busy. Idleness is never good for anyone."

"She used to get mad at us for if we were dawdling or wasting time," said Nucia. "But that was before…"

Rachel got up quickly when she saw her mother's eyes flicker. Since the riots, her eyes had been vacant, as if they understood nothing, recognized nobody. Now her mother's eyes roamed the room, as if seeing it for the first time. When she saw Rachel, she reached out and caressed her cheek.

"Mother," said Rachel softly.

Her mother's bony arms reached out for her. Rachel bent down into her embrace, feeling Nucia's arms around her as well. Her mother's eyes welled up with tears and a raw, guttural sound escaped from her throat. She began crying for the first time since they had arrived at the hospital, softly at first, then rising to an intense wail that reverberated off the walls. Her body shook as all of her anguish and despair emerged. Rachel and Nucia held onto their mother, their bodies moving with hers until the emotion within her subsided, and she was still.

"Are you all right?" asked Rachel.

"Girls, give your mother some room to breathe," said Rena, pulling them gently away from their mother.

"Yes, I believe I am all right," their mother replied weakly, propping herself up on her elbows. She gazed sadly at Rachel and Nucia. "I have not been a good mother…"

"Don't worry. We are just grateful to hear you speaking again," said Nucia. She and Rachel moved forward, away from Rena, and helped their mother sit up.

"I felt like I was in a dream, a nightmare really," she said. "Words and faces would appear in my head and then vanish. I could breathe, walk, move my head, but it was as if I was watching everyone else and couldn't join in."

"Dr. Slutskii believes you were in shock," said Rena, now standing at the foot of the cot. "There are many people here in the same condition."

"Like Chaia?" asked Rachel.

"Yes."

"Will she come out of shock, like Mother has?"

Rena shrugged her shoulders. "Hopefully, yes. But the doctor says some people take longer than others." She returned her attention to Rachel's mother. "Did you hear what I said about needing people to sew?"

"We can earn some money, Mother," said Nucia. "And you like to sew. You always tell me how proud you are to wear something you've made."

Rena moved around the cot and took hold of Rachel's mother's hand. "I know you are ready to help your daughters. They need you very much."

"Then I must stop mourning and move forward. He helps those who help themselves," she continued, her voice rough and dry. "We will be grateful for work as seamstresses. Thank you, Rena."

Rena cleared her throat and walked toward the door. "That's fine. I'll gather the supplies and orders. Come to Room 12 tomorrow morning to begin."

"Tomorrow is too soon," said Rachel's mother. "I don't know if I will be ready."

"We will help you, won't we Rachel?" said Nucia.

"Yes, of course…only…"

"What is it?" asked her mother.

Rachel sighed. "You know I'm hopeless with a needle and thread. I'm worried about sewing well enough for other people."

Her mother and Nucia shared a smile.

"You will be fine," Nucia promised. "I'll help you."

Rachel smiled, feeling closer to her sister than she'd ever been before.

❄❄❄

Rachel and Leah waited for Yoram to say good-bye to Chaia and then stood on each side of her bed. She was still bandaged from head to foot and hadn't spoken a word since the riots.

"Look Chaia," said Rachel. "I brought Leah to see you. She's had her hair cut, like you."

Leah's eyes darted from Rachel to Chaia. "So? How are you Chaia?" She scratched the back of her neck and continued in a shaky voice. "You should see me now." She laughed nervously. "I'm practically bald with a big scar on my face. I don't think any boys are going to want to marry me but that's all right…" She choked back tears and looked at Rachel.

"Don't worry about Leah," Rachel said, struggling to keep her voice from faltering. "She doesn't look so bad. The doctor told her the scar will eventually fade so you'll hardly notice it."

Chaia's eyes remained fixed on the ceiling, blinking occasionally but showing no sign that she heard them.

"You're looking much better, Chaia," said Rachel. "You have more color in your face and your bruises are almost gone." She took Chaia's hand, which was cold and limp. "It's not so bad in here. A bit crowded but it's clean." She inhaled. "Tomorrow I'm going with my mother and sister to start sewing clothes for…for people. You really have to wake up to see me with a needle and thread. I'll be lucky if I don't sew my hands together."

Leah laughed gently. "I will definitely come and watch you, Rachel. And I feel sorry for the people who get your clothes. They will likely fall apart."

Rachel peered at Chaia's face to see if her lips moved at all, maybe a hint of a smile. She shook her head at Leah.

Leah frowned. "Yoram really misses you. He was just here, do you know that?" She and Rachel stared at Chaia's face but saw no response.

"I miss you so much, Chaia," said Rachel. "So does Leah. And your mother, she is so sad that you aren't talking. We know you need time. I just hope that soon you'll come back to us." She let go of Chaia's hand and backed up, watching intently for any change in her expression. Nothing. She stifled a cry, then trudged out of the room with Leah.

❄❄❄

The gaslights cast an eerie fog onto the black streets. An afternoon rain had left the night air warm and moist. Sergei spied two officers down the street and hurried toward them. "Have you seen Chief Khanzhenkov?"

The officers eyed Sergei suspiciously. "Who wants to know?" one of them croaked.

"He's my father. He left for work early this morning and hasn't come home."

"Have you checked the station?" asked the other officer.

"I've already been there. Nobody's seen him all day." Sergei saw the two men exchange glances. "I know he's drinking somewhere. But there are a lot of taverns in town."

"Try the Moscow," the first officer replied. "If he's not there, try the Bear. Yes—that's what I'd do."

Sergei nodded in reply and headed down the street, anger churning his stomach. "Why does my father have to make such a fool of himself?" he muttered, his fists clenched.

Lights from the taverns, gambling dens, and restaurants glowed hazily as Sergei walked past open doors. The smell of alcohol and smoke assaulted his nose. Taking a deep breath, he entered the Moscow and found himself in the reddest room he'd ever seen. Lit sconces against crimson walls infused the floor with a ruby tinge. Thick red stripes ran along the edges of the tablecloths.

Tables of six were filled with men talking and laughing loudly over their drinks. A large archway led to another room, where the atmosphere was more subdued. At one table, the men were passed out, their heads on the table.

Tucked back in the darkest corner, he saw his father

hunched over a table with men Sergei didn't recognize. A gray cloud of smoke hovered above their heads.

"Papa..." Sergei glared at his father as he approached. "Papa!" he repeated in a louder voice.

Sergei's father raised his head and tried to focus his eyes on the source of the voice. "What...what the devil're you doing here?" His voice slurred.

"Mama is worried about you. She sent me to find you," Sergei replied tersely.

The other men peered at Sergei, their drunken eyes mere slits in their ruddy faces.

"Oh, for goodness sake. Can't a man have some time to himself?" Sergei's father grinned, raised his glass and proposed a toast. "Here's to...time with friends!"

He and the other men roared with laughter, and reached for their glasses.

"Are you coming home or not?" Sergei asked.

"When I'm good and ready."

"Hear, hear!" yelled one of his cronies. The three men clanged their glasses together in a toast. Sergei noticed his father's hand shake as he held his glass. Scowling, Sergei turned and left, sighing with relief when he was back outside. He savored the cool, clean air, but couldn't rid his mind of his father's drunken condition. He glanced back at the tavern, then walked toward lower Kishinev, with thoughts of Rachel crowding out the ugly images of his father.

Under the cloak of darkness, it was easy to forget about the massacre. Desecrated buildings were blotted out, hidden, unseen. The gaslights shining brightly in the night made the town appear picturesque, almost holy. Looming in front of him was the Jewish hospital. The stark building rose from the ground like a shadow.

"Sergei?"

Sergei turned and saw Rachel standing under a gaslight, her face partially concealed in the night's shadows.

"I couldn't sleep," she said. "When I closed my eyes, I saw… anyway, the lights shone through my window. At night I can pretend Kishinev is the same as it was. That it wasn't destroyed."

"I was thinking the same thing. But you shouldn't be out here alone. You could get hurt."

"I'm not afraid. Besides, I'm only a few steps from the hospital." She spoke matter-of-factly, with no emotion. "Have you seen Menahem since he was sent to the orphanage?"

"A couple of times. He's miserable. He spends most of his time doing chores, and there are fights. When I leave I feel terrible."

Rachel nodded. "When I'm sad about losing my father, I think of Menahem and how much worse off he is. I feel bad for feeling sorry for myself when I know there are so many children like him out there."

"I wish I could do more for him." Despair and anger flooded through Sergei. "I lie awake at night trying to make sense of everything." He grimaced and his voice rose. "Yet my father, who could have stopped the riots but didn't, sits in a tavern as we speak,drinking himself into a stupor as if nothing happened."

"It doesn't pay to be good."

"You're right."

"I should get back now, before my mother notices I'm gone." She waved and moved out of the light.

"Wait! Let me walk with you," Sergei called.

"It's all right," Rachel replied. "I'll be fine."

Sergei kept an eye on her until she disappeared into the misty night. After one last glance at the hospital, he went home.

❄❄❄

A group of children hovered near Sergei as he stood in the entry hall of the orphanage with Menahem. Like Menahem, they all had sad eyes and protruding cheekbones. Although Sergei knew there were lots of children in the orphanage, actually seeing their faces made him feel guilty for befriending just one.

"I guess we should go, Menahem." Sergei turned his head to the door to avoid the children's hopeful gazes and left with Menahem clinging tightly to his hand. "Does anybody ever come to visit those other children?" Sergei asked as they headed to Chuflinskii Square. "Were they all orphaned after the riots?"

Menahem put his finger to his lip as he pondered this question. "I don't know."

Sergei's eyes searched Menahem's face to make sure he wasn't upset talking about the massacre.

"Sometimes at night, I hear them cry out for their mothers and fathers."

"What about you?" asked Sergei. "Are things getting better now?"

"I still miss my grandmother. She used to make special latkes for me, even if it wasn't Hanukkah, and every night she told me a story before I went to sleep. She couldn't read but she had all kinds of stories in her head." Menahem's voice grew faint.

They arrived at the square, but Sergei wanted to keep

talking. Holding Menahem's hand, he guided him to the walkway around the perimeter of the square. "You've never told me what happened to your parents."

"They died when I was a baby. It was a fever that killed a lot of people. My grandmother's always taken care of me."

"Sergei!" Petya ran up to them from across the square. "Sergei...we're getting teams together for a game of *gorodki*. We're one short. Come and join us."

"Sorry, I can't. I'm with...I'm with my friend Menahem."

Petya spied Menahem hiding behind Sergei's back. "He can come too. The two of you can share the spot."

"I don't know how to play," Menahem said quietly.

"I can teach you, Menahem. It's a great game," said Sergei, thinking this would take Menahem's mind off his troubles.

"You throw a wooden baton at a town made up of towers of blocks," added Petya. "If you knock them down, you win."

Menahem backed away from them with round, frightened eyes.

"Oh no!" Sergei said, hitting his forehead as he realized what he'd done. "I can't believe we just asked him to play gorodki."

"What do you mean? What's wrong with gorodki?" asked Petya.

"Menahem's home was destroyed in the massacre here. By us."

"Wait a minute...I didn't destroy anybody's house," said Petya.

"We didn't exactly try to stop people either. And then what do we do? Ask him to play a game where we destroy a town." Sergei saw Menahem running back the way they'd come and started to chase him, overtaking him on the sidewalk. "Menahem, wait! I'm sorry. We were idiots. We weren't thinking. I'll make it up to you. I promise."

Menahem's face was streaked with dirty tears, which he tried to erase with the back of his hand. He was breathing heavily.

"Please. I made a mistake. I'm sorry."

"You're just like the rest of them," said Menahem.

"No, no, I'm not. I really hate the people who destroyed your house and the rest of the town. And I really like you. I come to visit you because I want to, not because I have to. You know that, don't you?" Sergei knelt down and took Menahem's hands.

Menahem nodded slowly. "I guess so."

Sergei smiled and hugged the boy. "If I had a brother, I'd want him to be just like you."

❄❄❄

Sergei opened the door and saw his mother on the sofa weeping and his father passed out at the table. An empty vodka bottle lay on its side near his head. Carlotta and Natalya were nowhere to be seen. He bent over his mother and spoke to her quietly. "Mama…what happened?"

She looked up at him. "Your father, he lost his position today." She started to cry again. Sergei put his arms around her, which only made her cry harder. "What are we going to do?"

"If he had done his job and not let those rioters ruin so many people's lives, this never would have happened." He pulled away from his mother.

"Sergei, don't talk that way about your father."

"You don't understand, do you? You don't see that he could have prevented the riots if only he'd arrested Mikhail's uncle and cousin. Instead, he let everyone in Kishinev think the murderer was Jewish. He let the hatred build and then stood back and did nothing while innocent people were beaten to death. I was there! I saw the police ignoring the rioters. Forty-nine Jews were killed and more than five hundred were injured. How can you defend him?" Sergei raised his voice louder than he intended, but saw from the corner of his eye that his father was still passed out.

"You don't know what you're saying, Sergei."

"I know exactly what I'm saying. There was even an article in the newspaper—about a document advising police to let the riots take place and not to help the Jews."

His mother gasped. "No, this can't be true. You're wrong."

Sergei shook his head. "It was written by the Russian Minister of the Interior, and it was called 'Perfectly Secret.' Papa says he was following orders, but if he was a good person, he would have ignored the stupid orders and helped the Jews."

Sergei's mother continued weeping into her hands.

He put his arm around her shoulder and held her until her crying subsided. "I'm sorry, Mama. I just thought you should know the truth."

❄❄❄

Hearing the rhythmic sound of his father's deep breathing punctuated by powerful snores, Sergei crept out of bed into the kitchen. He stopped when the floor creaked. Convinced that nobody in his house was awake, he walked gingerly to the shelf near the window. He picked up the birch-bark-and-iron coffer that sat there. The moon provided just enough light to see. Sergei lifted the lid and peered inside.

The coffer was filled with rubles and kopecks. He shoved half of the money into the leather pouch he wore around his waist, then put the coffer back in its place and quietly returned to bed.

MAY

Local Jews are doing their utmost to relieve the suffering. Young Jewesses are attending the sick in the hospitals and money is pouring in from all the Jewish communities in Russia. Twelve thousand persons are receiving two pounds of bread a day, and 2,500 portions are distributed at the soup kitchen daily, but this is a drop in the ocean.

—The Jewish Chronicle, *May 23, 1903*

One

Rachel ran into the room where Nucia and her mother sat with three other women at a long table sewing.

"It's here! A letter. An answer from Zeyde and Bubbe! Mother, Nucia!" Rachel held the letter up excitedly.

Nucia stopped working and stared at Rachel. Her mother looked up at her with a puzzled expression. The other three women glanced at Rachel and went back to their needles and thread.

"See!" Rachel said, waving the small white envelope in the air. "Rena just handed it to me."

"You wrote to them?" asked her mother. "When did you write this letter?"

"A few weeks ago." Rachel's fingers fumbled as she ripped apart the envelope. "I didn't tell you—in case they didn't write back."

"I can't believe they actually responded," said Nucia. She

set her sewing down and looked eagerly at Rachel. "Aren't you going to read it?"

Her fingers shook as she pulled the note out of the envelope and lifted her eyes to her mother and Nucia.

"What is it?" asked her mother.

"There...there are tickets in here!"

Nucia furrowed her brow. "Tickets? What kind of tickets?"

Rachel swallowed and took them out. "Train tickets. To Vladivostock. From Kishinev."

"Why would we go there?" asked her mother. "They live in Gomel."

"I don't know," said Rachel, her eyes scanning the letter for details. She began to read it out loud, her lips curling up into a broad smile as she reached the end of the letter.

Rachel,

We were overcome with grief when we read your letter. Gofsha was our only son and our hearts are in pain from our sadness and regret. Our stubbornness has cost us dearly. Bubbe has taken the news especially hard. She has been quite ill, but her condition has improved slightly and for that we are grateful.

Though we long to see you and to know you, we must put your safety ahead of our wishes. There is talk of a riot here, so you must go to the eastern port of Vladivostok, the gateway to Shanghai and America. Take a steamer or a freighter to Shanghai, where they accept us without papers, without hatred. From there, you can travel to a new life in America. Enclosed, please find three tickets to Vladivostok. I wish I could send you enough money

for your passage to America, but this is all I have. Please let us know when you have arrived in your new home,
Zeyde

Rachel's mother let out a big sigh. "This is too much... train tickets are expensive. They need the money for Bubbe."

"They wouldn't have purchased the tickets for us if they couldn't afford it," said Rachel, her eyes moving from her mother to Nucia.

"America," said Nucia, her eyes shining.

"It is so far from here, from everything we know," said Rachel's mother, her voice breaking as she spoke.

"What would Father do?" Rachel gazed at her mother for a response.

The other three women stopped sewing and stared at Rachel's mother—all of them now quiet and pensive.

Rachel's mother turned and gazed out the small window facing the courtyard. It was open to let in the fresh spring air, and the dull murmur of voices drifted up.

"He would want us to be safe," Rachel's mother said finally, her eyes still on the window. "He would want us to do as Zeyde says." She turned back to Rachel and Nucia and spoke in a strained voice that lacked the strength and vigor it had once possessed. "I know he would want us to go to America."

"You are so lucky, Ita," said one of their sewing companions. "And you must think of your girls."

"Yes," added another. "You must go. These tickets are a blessing."

"Yes...but we still need to earn money for the ship's passage," said Rachel's mother brusquely, signaling the end of the conversation. She took the tickets from Rachel and placed them in the cloth pouch that she wore around her neck. "Let us continue our work, Nucia. And Rachel," she waved at a neat pile of fabric on one end of the table, "there is plenty for you to do, yes?"

Rachel sat down beside her mother and resumed sewing the chemise she'd been working on for hours. Excited by the news, she worked as quickly as she could, determined to make the money they needed as soon as possible. But her carelessness caused mistakes, one so large that she had to rip out an entire seam.

"Ech!" she groaned as she pulled at the threads in the coarse fabric.

"Patience, Rachel," warned her mother. "Or you will have nothing to show for your efforts today."

"I know. I just wish I could sew as well as you and Nucia."

"In time," said her mother. "In time."

"I can't wait to be out of this hospital on our way to America," said Nucia. "Mother, did Father ever tell you about his parents?"

Their mother stopped sewing and rested her hands on the table. She had a faraway look in her eyes. "A little…it made him sad. He told me his father was very smart but very stubborn, and his mother was always frail."

"I wonder if we'll ever meet them." Rachel sighed. "I wish they could come to America with us."

Her mother pressed her lips together and resumed sewing. "From Zeyde's letter, it is clear Bubbe is not well enough to make such a long journey."

"But what will happen to them if there are riots in Gomel?" asked Nucia.

Rachel saw her mother's back stiffen, but she didn't take her eyes off her work. Neither did the other women. Rachel's heart sank. Her grandparents could end up homeless, or worse.

❄❄❄

Rachel shrugged her shoulders to release the tension. They were stiff from being hunched over her sewing all day. When she dropped her empty soup bowl into the bucket, Rachel glanced at her mother and sister who were still eating. "I'm going to take a walk," she announced. "I'll meet you back at the hospital."

"Should you be outside by yourself?" asked her mother.

"I'll be fine. The days are longer now, and I need to stretch my legs," she replied, stepping back from her mother. Rachel had noticed a change in their relationship since her mother had regained her awareness. She no longer admonished Rachel for small things, and she trusted her judgment, as if Rachel had suddenly gone from being fourteen to sixteen. "I've been sitting so long today," Rachel called back as she was leaving. "I almost feel like sleeping on my feet tonight."

Rachel headed down the street without a backward glance. She craved time alone. It was something she'd taken for granted before the massacre, being curled up by the stove with a good book. Now the former world seemed far away.

Though some of the debris had been removed, there were still constant reminders of the hatred that had prevailed. And when she took a deep breath to revel in the warm spring air, it was the scent of decay that she smelled.

Almost every store she passed had been pillaged or

destroyed. Rachel wondered how the town would ever recover from so much damage.

At the river, Rachel found herself on the same path she had taken the day Mikhail was killed. Today, however, there was no snow or ice. Instead, mud caked the weathered felt boots that pinched her toes, and trees and lilac shrubs dense with new leaves and blooms made it hard to see where she was going. As she moved further away from the street, the air grew fragrant with lilacs and the mud became thicker, like the dough her mother used to knead when she made black bread.

At one point, her foot sank in the thick sludge, stopping Rachel in her tracks. "Oh no!" She groaned as she pulled her boot from the mud. Moving carefully to avoid the clumps of muck, Rachel kept her eyes on the path until she reached the trees by the River Byk.

I have to do this, she told herself, as she hesitated. I have to be able to face my demons before I leave Kishinev behind forever. She walked out from the trees and stood by the bench—the last place she had seen Mikhail. No longer frozen, the river was greenish-brown and barely flowing. It looked dirty and much less inviting than it did in the winter when it was shiny and white.

She brushed some dried leaves and dirt off the bench and sat down. The hairs on the back of her neck stood up as she remembered the last time she'd been here. She could still picture Mikhail skating on the ice, his face so full of life and promise.

"Rachel?"

Startled, she turned and saw Sergei standing behind the bench. She smiled. "I guess we both had the same idea today."

Sergei sat down beside her. "Not really. I saw you walking in this direction and followed you."

She blushed.

Sergei sat down. "I come here often. I like to get away from everyone, and this seems to be the only place in Kishinev that wasn't destroyed."

Rachel nodded. "This is the first time I've been back since…since…" She looked out at the river.

"I know," said Sergei quietly.

"Kishinev will never be the same. I'm glad we're leaving soon." Rachel picked up a stone and threw it in the river.

"You're leaving? When?"

"When we can raise enough money for a ship's passage to America. My grandparents sent us train tickets to Vladivostok."

Sergei nodded and fidgeted with the stones he held in his hands. "America…that will be a long journey."

Rachel nodded and picked up some stones. "I've never been away from Kishinev. It's hard to imagine living so far away, in another country." She pitched the stones into the water and listened to the plunking sound they made as they sank.

Sergei looked at her closely, studying her face as if he would never see her again. "Will you write to me? I've always wanted to know what it's like in America."

She gave him a half-smile. "Of course." Her eyes moved to the river again, to the spot where she had last seen Mikhail. "And I'm going to write about Kishinev." She turned and looked at Sergei. "So that people don't forget what really happened to Mikhail and my father."

He grinned. "You will be a famous writer when your story is published. I'm sure of it."

Rachel felt warm and happy hearing the conviction in

Sergei's voice. He made her feel like anything was possible, that her dreams really could come true.

"Mikhail and I had plans to travel to Petersburg together." He threw a stone, which skipped lightly over the water. "I was going to study art and Mikhail planned to work there and go to the university." Sergei pushed the mud around with his feet and scowled. "But now…my father lost his job and is drinking our savings away."

Rachel turned and stared at him. "Your father is not the police chief anymore?"

He shook his head and smiled grimly. "He got what he deserved. Only it means I have to get a job to help take care of my mother and my sister and aunt." He played with a stone in his hand and tossed it into the river. "Everyone—everything—has changed. The whole town is a different place now. I feel like I'm twenty years older than I was, as if I have the world on my shoulders." He sighed and bit his lip. "Especially when I'm out looking for a job and my father is drunk at the tavern." He looked pointedly at Rachel. "I love him because he's my father, but I despise him as well. That sounds strange, doesn't it?"

"No, it doesn't." She paused. "Does he know you want to be an artist?"

Sergei grunted. "He thinks I'm going to become a police officer like he was."

"Will you ever tell him the truth?"

"Probably not." He shrugged. "It was a stupid idea. I haven't had time to draw in weeks. I need to make money now."

"I don't think it's stupid. Maybe you'll get a chance to become an artist someday."

He hurled a large stone into the muddy water. "I doubt it."

"Can your aunt get a job to help?"

He laughed. "She's not right in the head. She says strange things to people, which is why she's never been married or able to work."

"That's a shame." Rachel picked up a small black stone and examined it closely in her hand. "I miss playing chess with my father. He taught me to play, and I thought I would beat him some day. Do you play?"

"A little, probably not as well as you. I don't have a lot of patience. I play a lot of backgammon, especially with my sister. Most of the time I let her win."

Rachel nodded and stared at the river. The setting sun cast a glowing red haze on the water. "I guess I'd better go now, before my mother gets worried," she said. "She's convinced another riot is about to occur."

"First..." Sergei reached into his leather pouch. "I want you to have this." He held out the money he had taken from the coffer.

"Where did you get that?"

"It doesn't matter. Just take it. You can use it for your passage to America."

She pressed her lips together and pushed his hand back, touched that he would make such a generous offer. Though she was determined to keep a wall between them that would guard her emotions, he was making it difficult. In spite of her best efforts, Rachel found herself caring for him. "No. I can't. My mother would ask questions, and it's not right. Your family needs it."

"But I want *you* to have it."

She shook her head firmly and stood up.

Sergei sighed again and returned the money to his pouch. "I'll walk with you." He stood and they followed the path to the street together.

Two

"I promised Leah I'd meet her in the courtyard," Rachel told her mother and sister. It was late afternoon and the three of them had finished sewing for the day. She left without waiting for them to respond, hurried outside where the air was cool, and sat down wearily on the top step. It had rained most of the morning, and the air felt heavy.

Rachel was stretching her arms above her head to loosen her cramped muscles when a tall stranger entered the hospital's courtyard. He had a thick beard, black as coal, and hair that stood straight up from his head.

"Mr. Korolenko…welcome," said Dr. Slutskii, the senior doctor who took care of Chaia and many other injured people in the hospital. He walked past Rachel and greeted the stranger. They shook hands and then the man called Korolenko opened a bag hanging over his shoulder, reached in, and pulled out a small notebook. He listened intently to Dr. Slutskii and wrote quickly. Rachel tried to listen, but they spoke in quiet voices.

Dr. Slutskii appeared to be talking about the hospital. He waved his arms around, pointed at the building, and was very animated. Rachel slid down to the bottom step and craned her neck to hear, but still couldn't make out one word. After a few moments, the two men walked by, nodding politely at Rachel as they passed, and entered the hospital.

As soon as they had disappeared through the door, Rachel raced back inside and found Rena in her office. "Who was that man?" she asked.

Rena looked up wearily from the stack of papers in front of her. "You mean the one who just came in with Dr. Slutskii?"

"Yes…"

"I believe that's Vladimir Korolenko, a journalist. He's come here to write about the massacre."

"A writer? You mean for newspapers?"

"I suppose so. Does it matter?"

Rachel's heart was pounding. "Didn't you read the newspapers? All those horrible lies about us?" Her voice rose as she spoke. "That we eat blood, that we want to take over Kishinev, that our corpses should be bound to the wheels of carts?"

Rena dropped the stack of papers she was holding onto her desk. "But Mr. Korolenko didn't write those things. You can't blame one writer for the poisonous pen of others."

Rachel's eyes blazed. "But how can you be so sure *he'll* write the truth?"

Rena sighed and reached out to hold Rachel's trembling hands. "Mr. Korolenko came here to find out what happened. To discover the facts, not to distort the truth. Dr. Slutskii says he has a very good reputation."

Rachel pulled away. "But," her eyes teared up, "he might change Dr. Slutskii's words for his story. How can you trust that he'll write about what *really* happened?"

Rena stood up, walked around her desk, and embraced Rachel. "I know you're scared," she said softly. "And I know it's hard for you to trust anyone...but you can't go through life in fear."

Rachel nodded and brushed the tears from her eyes as Leah walked into the office. Her hair was starting to grow back, but the scar on her face was now an ugly purple line, a constant reminder of the riots. "There you are. I thought we were going to meet in the courtyard," she began. "Oh, what's wrong, Rachel?"

"She's fine, nothing to worry about," answered Rena quickly. "I have an idea. Rachel, would you like to read to a group of children? I was going to, but I have so much work. I have a few books somewhere." Rena rummaged through a wooden box and pulled out a couple of books covered in dust. "Here we are. And since Leah still gets headaches when she reads, she can listen too."

Before she could protest, Rachel found herself sitting on the courtyard steps surrounded by at least one hundred children of all ages. She cleared her throat, looked at Leah sitting off to the side, and held out the book so the children could see the cover. "Russian Fairy Tales by Verra Xenophontovna," she began in a feeble voice.

"Louder," said Leah.

Rachel nodded and opened the book. The crisp pages were like long-lost friends. She cherished their smoothness, the smart way they sounded when she turned them, and the delightful smell of words made of ink.

"Baba Yaga." Rachel showed the children the picture, then

started to read from the first page. Suddenly she remembered that the story was about two children whose mother had died.

"Ei! Maybe this is not such a good choice," she said, leafing through the pages. "Here's another—Woe Bogotir."

Rachel began to read. "*In a small village—do not ask me where; in Russia, anyway—there lived two brothers; one of them was rich, the other poor. The rich brother had good luck in everything he undertook, was always successful, and had a profit out of every venture. The poor brother, in spite of all his trouble and all his work, had none whatever.*"

Rachel looked up and saw the children's eyes fastened on her. She continued reading, pausing once in a while to clear her throat. Just as she was about to start the last page, she sensed someone watching her from behind. Turning around, she saw the journalist, Korolenko, regarding her with serious, dark brown eyes. Rachel felt awkward under his gaze, and tried, unsuccessfully, to ignore him as she finished the story. She stuttered, tripping on words, gratefully closing the book when the story was finished.

"So you see, the lesson in this story is if you treat people kindly, you can expect good luck to follow," she told the children.

"Rachel, the rich brother treated people badly and ended up with bad luck. Isn't that right?" asked a young girl. She was about ten or eleven years old and had sat with her hands clasped together the entire time Rachel had been reading.

"Yes."

"Well," the girl continued, "will the people who hurt us end up with bad luck?"

"Yes." A tall, thin boy with freckles spoke up. "My father says they're going to jail."

Rachel glanced over at Korolenko and saw him writing furiously on his notepad, while Dr. Slutskii stood nearby with his arms crossed. "That's right. They will be punished."

"But most of us didn't do anything bad," said another boy, who looked older than the rest of the children, "so how come we've had such bad luck?"

A little girl nodded and added, "My mother told me it doesn't pay to be good."

Rachel shuddered, recalling her conversation with Sergei when she had said the exact same words.

The children started arguing amongst themselves, their voices getting louder and louder.

"If my father was here, he'd remind me about one of Sholem Aleichem's stories," said Rachel loudly enough to be heard over the children. "When the character Tevye discovers his daughter loves a gentile, he thinks about the differences between Jews and gentiles. He wonders why there are Jews and non-Jews. Why should one be so cut off from the other? And why should they be unable to look at one another, when they are from the same place?"

"What did Tevye decide?" asked Leah.

"He realized he didn't know the answer," said Rachel. "And I suppose nobody really does. If they did, maybe we all wouldn't be here right now." She glanced back at Korolenko. He was writing quickly, his pen moving fluidly across the paper. Rachel glanced up and met his dark eyes. She wondered what he was thinking and what he would end up writing. Even though Rena was sure this man was honorable, Rachel was not convinced.

❄❄❄

Rachel heard Chaia's laughter. It was coming from behind her but when she turned around, nobody was there. Everything was green. The trees, the grass. Spring was everywhere. There was the laughter again. Rachel turned in a circle. Her father's violin played a haunting melody she'd never heard before.

"Sholom aleichem."

"Sacha! Sacha Talinsky, where are you?" she called. Her voice echoed.

"It serves you right," said Nucia's voice, which seemed to float above her like a cloud.

Rachel looked up, but the sky was clear and bluer than she'd ever seen.

"Where is everyone? Why are you hiding?" Rachel cried. "Come out, let me see you."

She walked and the green started to become a murky yellow. The trees lost their leaves and the wind began whistling by. Rachel crossed her arms and shivered.

Mikhail's voice suddenly interrupted the silence. "Stop! Please don't!"

Rachel covered her ears to keep Mikhail's words out of her head. She began running until the sky was gray and snow was falling. Chaia's face appeared before her, staring at her with blank eyes.

She stopped running and looked around. A path led to the right, where an arch of barren trees seemed to be waiting for her. Rachel began walking, but stopped when she heard wolves howling in the distance.

"Help!" she cried. "Help! Please, someone help me."

A crashing noise sounded from in front of her. Rachel froze in place. There was a river, with three large objects floating in it. Rachel tiptoed closer until she could see they were heads. She screamed. The heads turned in the water, revealing the faces of Mikhail, her father, and Mr. Berlatsky. All three faces smiled at her.

"No!" screamed Rachel. "No!"

"Wake up! Wake up, Rachel, you're having a nightmare."

Rachel opened her eyes when she heard her mother's voice. She pulled the cover over her face, expecting to see her mother's head bobbing in the river.

Her mother pulled the cover down. "It's all right. You were having a bad nightmare."

Wearily, she turned her head away, but when she closed her eyes, she saw the river again, with the heads floating on its surface. The rest of the night Rachel lay awake with her eyes wide open, waiting for daylight to obscure her nightmare.

Three

A soft cry woke Sergei. The flat was bathed in early morning light. He sat up slowly and remained sitting on the side of his bed until the grogginess subsided.

His mother sat at the kitchen table staring blankly out the window. As his eyes cleared, he saw that she was still wearing the clothes she had on the previous day. She looked exhausted. Rachel was right. His mother needed money right now. He tiptoed over to the coffer and replaced the money he'd taken.

"Mama, didn't you sleep?" Sergei sat down beside her and tapped her lightly on the shoulder. "Mama?"

"Your father didn't come home last night," she said. Only her lips moved as she spoke, and she looked old and tired, her skin ashen gray.

"He probably lost track of time at the tavern, Mama. He'll be home soon." Sergei wrapped his right arm loosely around her shoulder.

She patted his hand. "You're a good boy, Sergei. A good boy."

He flushed with embarrassment.

"Your father…he used to be good also. Honest. Smart. But somehow he lost his way. I don't know how it happened, or when."

"It's all right Mama. You don't have to talk about—"

"Hush." His mother interrupted with an urgency that surprised him. "I must talk. I don't want *you* to lose your way."

"I'll stay with you, Mama, so that I don't lose my way." He was surprised by the words that had slipped so easily from his lips.

"No! That's not what I mean. You must go far away from here—where you can escape your father's reputation, where you can start fresh."

A few months ago, this was exactly what he had wanted, but now he wasn't so sure. He didn't want to leave his mother and sister behind.

"I have something for you." His mother stood up, walked to the cupboard, and took out the coffer.

Sergei held his breath as she pulled off the lid and took out the money he had just returned. "Here. Take this." She pushed the rubles and kopecks into his hand.

Sergei pushed it back. "You need it for yourself and Natalya and Carlotta. I can't take it."

His mother fixed her teary eyes on his. "There is still enough money for us, and I have found work as a seamstress. We'll be fine."

Sergei stared at the money, which lay heavy in his hand.

"Put it in a safe place where your father won't find it. He's squandering everything he has on cards and drink. Go. Make haste. Hide it safely away."

He hugged his mother tightly. Now he could go away with his mother's blessing. Still, his throat constricted as he thought about leaving Natalya with his drunken father. And he worried about leaving Menahem all alone in the orphanage. But if he stayed, it would be hard to find work with his father's tarnished reputation. There was no perfect solution, no easy answer.

❄❄❄

Curious eyes peered around the corner as Sergei waited for Menahem. He attempted to smile at the children watching him, but his mouth refused to cooperate.

"Hello, Sergei!" Menahem beamed when he saw him, making Sergei feel even guiltier about the prospect of abandoning the boy.

As Menahem moved closer, Sergei noticed a lump on his forehead. "What happened to you?"

Menahem looked down at the floor. "Nothing. It's all right. Can we just go?"

Sergei searched for the matron, hoping for an answer, but she was busy tending to a weeping child.

As soon as they were out of the courtyard, Sergei stopped walking and took hold of Menahem. "We're away from the orphanage. Now, tell me what happened. How did you get that lump?"

"There's this group of big boys," Menahem answered slowly, "and when they tell us to do something, we have to do it, or they hit us." He took a deep breath. "This one, named Ivan, told me to steal the matron's key so he could go into the kitchen at night for food. I couldn't do it. If you get in trouble, you have to sleep in a dark room all by yourself. I was afraid of being caught."

"That's horrible! When did he hit you?"

"When I was asleep last night. But it doesn't hurt too much."

Sergei groaned. "Didn't the matron punish him?"

"I didn't tell her. If I did, Ivan would keep hitting me."

"But…your head?"

"She's too busy to notice." Menahem looked up at Sergei. "Don't tell her. It'll be worse for me if you do."

Sergei sighed. "I promise. Come. Let's get something to eat." How could he ever say good-bye to Menahem, when the people who were supposed to be looking after him didn't care about him.

"You look sad today," said Menahem as they waited in line at a street vendor.

Sergei forced a smile. "I might have to go away."

"From Kishinev?"

Sergei nodded. "I need to find a job. There's nothing here."

Menahem's eyes brimmed with tears.

Sergei averted his eyes to keep from changing his mind. "What would you like to eat?" he asked.

"I'm not hungry." Menahem turned and walked away.

Sergei followed. "I know that's not true. You get barely enough to survive at the orphanage." Menahem kept walking. Sergei grabbed his shirtsleeve and stopped him. "Talk to me, Menahem."

"What do you care about what I eat? You're leaving." Menahem pulled away from Sergei.

Sergei pictured him covered in bumps and bruises from boys at the orphanage and flinched. "Don't be mad," he said. "I'm not leaving yet."

Menahem peered at him. "Do you mean it? You're really not going away?"

Sergei bit his bottom lip and nodded. "Not right away," he said. He would keep trying to get work in Kishinev so he could watch over Menahem, and take care of his mother and sister. It was crazy, thinking he could just leave as if this boy meant nothing to him.

❄❄❄

Sergei woke abruptly to the sound of breaking glass. He shook his head and touched his money pouch to make sure it was still there. Running his hand through his messy hair, he stood up and stretched. Outside his window the night was heavy and black.

Sergei heard a loud smash in the front room. Afraid that his family was being robbed, he walked cautiously from his bedroom, grabbing the heavy drinking cup from his bedside table to throw at an intruder if necessary. But the only person in the living area was his father, who gazed at him with hollow eyes from the sofa. Sergei entered the room and just missed stepping on a broken vodka bottle.

His father belched and kicked a glass tumbler lying at his feet.

"When are you going to stop drinking and get a job?" he asked his father. "How can you expect Mama, Natalya, and Carlotta to put up with this?"

"Do you have a cigarette?" his father asked, searching the

room to find one. Sergei saw despair in his eyes, which frightened him. He hardly recognized his father anymore. It was as if a stranger had taken over his body and mind—a curse for not helping the Jews during the riots. Sergei trudged back to bed, where he lay awake for the rest of the night.

❄❄❄

Rachel smiled when she saw Sergei waiting for her in the crowded hospital courtyard. "What are you doing here?" she asked.

He grinned and handed her a leather-bound journal full of empty pages. "If you're going to write about Kishinev, you'll need lots of paper."

She looked down at the journal and cradled it in her arms, against her chest. "Thank you. This is a wonderful gift." Her eyes glistened.

Sergei nodded and glanced at the entry to the courtyard. "I've been turned down for jobs at three cabinet makers, four shopkeepers, and a wax chandler today." He paused. "So I'm hoping you can go for a walk and cheer me up."

Rachel fell in step with him. "I know what you're feeling. If you watched me sew, you'd be laughing in no time," she said as they strolled out of the courtyard. "I spend more time getting rid of knots in the thread, and then re-threading the needle, than I do sewing. Fortunately, my mother and sister are making much better progress, or we'd never make enough money for our passage."

"I know you'll be safer in America, but I wish you weren't leaving."

Rachel blushed. "Maybe you'll come to America one day and visit me." She twisted her braid. "I hope you come."

He stopped and touched her shoulder while people rushed by, jostling them as they stood in the middle of the sidewalk. In the distance, she heard the sweet sound of a *balalaika*. Her heart fluttered with the music.

"It's too crowded here. Where do you want to go?" he asked.

"I don't know. The river?"

"A group of my friends are there." He lowered his eyes. "It might not be such a good idea."

"You're right…wait a minute! There's another section of the river that hardly anybody knows about," Rachel said. "Your friends won't be anywhere near us. Come on."

Rachel led Sergei past deserted makeshift shanties into a forest of towering spruce trees.

"We're almost there," she said, breathing in the savory aroma of wild mushrooms that lined their path. The ground was flat, wet, and green as they approached the river.

"I can't believe how narrow the river is here," Sergei said.

Rachel shaded her eyes and squinted. "You can hop to the other side. I haven't been here in ages." She pointed to a spot at the river's edge. "Look, the ground is pretty dry over there."

She ran to the spot and sat down. Sergei did the same, sitting close so that their arms touched. Rachel gazed ahead dreamily. "Sometimes I wish I could just live in a place like this, with no other people around to tell me what to do or say."

She turned and met his eyes. Chills ran up her spine as his face moved closer and his lips met hers. They were warm and his breath smelled of tobacco and mint, which reminded her of Mikhail. Rachel pulled away. "We shouldn't be doing this," she said.

"Why not?"

"Because I'm Jewish, and you're not. Because if anyone saw you with me, they'd kill me, and maybe even you. I think that's why Mikhail's uncle killed him—"

"Because you were friends? You think his uncle killed him because of you?"

She nodded and looked away.

"That's not true, Rachel. His uncle had just lost his job as a policeman. Mikhail's grandfather believes he wanted to inherit his business—for the money. The indictment against Mikhail's uncle was published in the newspaper today. The trial is tomorrow. Here," he said, pulling a square piece of paper out of his coat pocket, "this pass will allow you to attend the trial. I would go, but I have to look for a job."

Rachel stared at Sergei as she tried to make sense of his words. "You mean…it wasn't my fault?" She took the pass and studied it carefully.

"That's exactly what I mean." He moved closer, so that their noses were almost touching. "Would it be all right if I kissed you again?"

Rachel held her breath and considered this. She felt a twinge of guilt for betraying Mikhail, but he was gone, and she'd never had deep feelings for him, not like these feelings she had for Sergei. Besides, she would be leaving soon. What harm could a kiss do?

She nodded, unable to tear her gaze from his. Sergei brushed a stray hair from her eyes and cupped her face in his hands. Their lips met, and he pulled her closer, wrapping his arms around her.

She trembled and pressed against him so tightly she could

feel his heart beating. "I guess Rena was right. I do need to start trusting people again," she said when they drew apart.

"Who's Rena?" He sounded out of breath.

"A very smart lady at the hospital." Rachel kissed him on the lips and smiled as he ran his fingers down her cheek. She felt his strong arms around her and wished she could hold onto this moment forever. Sergei had been so good to her, and to Menahem, which she knew would have impressed her father. It was going to be hard leaving him, but even if she stayed, they had no future. A Jew and a gentile could never be together.

A magpie began chattering noisily overhead, breaking the silence. They started back toward the hospital, hands by their sides so that their deepening relationship would remain a secret.

❄❄❄

"Rachel...a letter came for you today." Rena held up an envelope as Rachel walked past her office.

"Who would write to me?" Rachel entered Rena's office reluctantly. She wanted to be alone to think about every moment she'd just spent with Sergei, to close her eyes and remember the way his hand felt on her face.

"Why don't you open it and see." Rena handed her the envelope and smiled.

Rachel unfolded the letter.

Dear Rachel,
Sholom aleichem! I hope this letter finds you well. We arrived in Petersburg a few days ago. It was a long, uneventful journey, and we are grateful to have a place

to stay. My aunt has been splendid, stuffing us with bread and fish and stew until we feel as if we might burst. My father looks much better now and is searching for a position.

You would love this city. There is so much to see, I feel a bit overwhelmed. You must keep your wits about you, for people are always in a hurry and travel quickly by carriage. I discovered these carriages take precedence on the streets when a horse almost took a bite of my overcoat!

My favorite place is the bookseller, where the books are stacked from the floor to the ceiling! I've never seen so many books in one place before! I have to be careful, because I don't have money to pay for one. So I browse as if I am going to buy, and then leave when the shopkeeper is helping someone else. Someday I'll be able to buy as many books as I like.

I want to attend the University of Petersburg, but Jews are not welcome, so all I can do is hope for a miracle. It's just as Tevye says, "a cow can sooner jump over a roof than a Jew get into a Russian university!"

Please record my address and write to me when you can.

—Sacha

Rachel folded the letter in half. Life would be so much easier if she cared for Sacha the way she cared for Sergei. She pictured herself kissing Sacha and chuckled. There was no way she could ever think of him as anything other than a good friend, and pretending would be wrong. Now that Sacha knew how she felt, he could meet someone who returned his feelings.

She sighed and made her way down the hall toward to the stairs. It disappointed Rachel that Sacha wasn't able to attend the university. She hoped it would be different in America, that Jews would not be banned from education and jobs, and that the long journey ahead would be worth the trouble and expense.

"Good afternoon Rachel." Mrs. Berlatsky was walking toward her.

"Good afternoon," said Rachel. "How is Chaia?"

A shadow crossed Mrs. Berlatsky's face. "The same. Her bones are mending well but her mind is somewhere else. We must remain here until she is better."

Tears welled up in Rachel's eyes. "I miss her. There is so much I need to tell her…" Mrs. Berlatsky patted her on the arm. "I'm sure your visits are helping her. One of these days she will be strong enough to come out of the world she's locked in now."

❄❄❄

Chaia is still a prisoner in her own body, which makes me feel guilty for surviving the massacre without injury. What she saw must have been a great shock for her eyes and her heart, but I know Chaia. She is strong and will wake up one day. I just hope that I am still here when she does, and not on my way to America.

Rachel stopped writing and frowned. This was her first entry in the journal she'd received from Sergei, and she was nervous about pouring her thoughts out again, taking the risk that they might be found and read. She looked down at what she had written. This was a chance she had to take.

The unfairness of life disturbs me. It makes no sense, how some are lucky and others, people like Chaia who are so good, have such bad luck.

❄❄❄

Rachel pushed her way through the dense crowd at the courtroom doors and showed her pass to the guard. She entered the building where the trial would be held, and found herself in a large square hall between two lines of guards. Seeing all the people—Jews and gentiles—in one large room, made her want to turn around and run back to the safety of the hospital. But she had to do this for Mikhail and for her father. She had to see justice done before she could start a new life without the anger that rumbled inside of her.

She took a seat at the end of a bench in the third row of the room. It was so crowded that only half of her bottom fit on the bench. Using her left leg, Rachel supported herself and waited for the trial to begin.

At ten o'clock, she heard a deep voice cry out, "Court is in session." A side door opened and twelve elderly senators walked in, boasting medals on their chests that reflected their many years of service to the Tsar. They took their seats in armchairs and a second side door opened.

Rachel gasped when she saw Mikhail's uncle and cousin enter, escorted by police officers. Both were well dressed and clean-shaven, which made them appear less threatening than on that fateful day when she had seen them with Mikhail. As her eyes grazed the rest of the spectators, she saw Mikhail's grandparents sitting directly behind the barrier. Though she'd never met them, the similarity between Mikhail and his grandfather was unmistakable. She studied their lined faces and thought sadly that Mikhail would never be a father or grandfather, nor reach old age.

The prosecutor read the indictment accusing Vasily and Philip Rybachenko of murder. Father and son remained stoic as the charge was read aloud. For the next hour, the prosecutor described in detail Mikhail's relationship to the accused, and how cards and drink led up to the murder. He spoke poignantly about how Mikhail's murder had altered his grandparents' lives, and stated that justice must be done to fully honor Mikhail's memory. He finished his speech recommending that the uncle be punished with the full force of the law and that Philip be given a lesser punishment because of his age.

Rachel's eyes moved to Mikhail's grandparents, who sat stone-faced. The administrator of the Kishinev Circuit Court, Goremykin, was a large man with dark whiskers. He announced that there would be an hour's recess before the defense spoke. Most people filed out for the break, but Rachel was content to remain in the hall to ensure she missed nothing. She felt a faint hunger pang but put it out of her mind by imagining herself on a ship to America, surrounded by clear water and a brilliant blue sky.

The courtroom filled up quickly after the break, and Rachel had been able to secure a better spot on the bench, closer to the middle. The tall, angular defense lawyer wasted no time, standing and making a case for his clients. He began by describing Vasily's childhood, how his father had clearly favored Mikhail's father. This feeling of inadequacy and rejection had followed him all his life, the lawyer emphasized, causing him to overindulge in spirits and cards. Not being asked to help run the family tobacco processing business was devastating, he continued, but he found solace in his position as a police officer and had only just been relieved of his duties two days before the murder. He was not desperate, and he had no animosity toward his young nephew, Mikhail. Furthermore, there were no witnesses to corroborate the prosecution's story, only hearsay, which was why he asked that the charges against his clients be dismissed.

The court broke into an agitated roar of disapproval. Rachel cowered in her seat as she listened to people shout out, "They're innocent," and "Why is there a trial without witnesses?" She looked over at the senators to see their reaction, but their faces remained passive, even bored.

She peered at Goremykin, pleading silently with him to put an end to the commotion, but he sat perfectly still for a number of minutes before he called for order. Then he asked the prosecutor if, in fact, he had a witness.

The prosecutor slowly got to his feet and shook his head. Voices rose instantly, calling for this farce to be over with, while others pleaded that the court consider the evidence. Rachel's heart clenched as she gazed around the courtroom. If she didn't come forward, Mikhail's killers would be freed. There would be no justice for Mikhail. She recalled her father's words, about knowing the right time to reveal her secret. She rose to her feet. Without hesitation, she walked to the front of the room, not entirely sure of what she was doing or what she would say. Her feet seemed to move separately from her body, thrusting her forward. As she drew nearer to Goremykin, the room became eerily silent. Her eyes did not waver from his face as she stood in front of him.

"I saw it," she began in a faint voice. "I saw Mikhail's uncle and cousin stab him on the river." She paused to take a deep breath. "I saw everything."

The courtroom erupted into a frenzy of shouting with accusations flying past Rachel from every direction. But she did not take her eyes off Goremykin, who shifted uncomfortably under her gaze.

"Enough!" he cried, looking beyond Rachel at the spectators. The room quietened down. "Who are you?" he asked.

"Rachel Paskar," she answered. "I was a friend of Mikhail's. I skated with him on the day...right before...he died."

He nodded for her to continue.

"I left, but forgot my shawl by the river and was going back to get it when I saw Mikhail talking with two men. Then I heard Mikhail call for help, and I hid behind a tree. He called the man 'uncle' and the boy 'Philip.' I did not hear much of their conversation, only Mikhail's cries for help. I saw his uncle pull a knife out of his pocket and stab Mikhail." Her voice broke but she was determined to finish. "Then Philip kicked him while his uncle kept stabbing him."

She lowered her eyes for a second, then raised them again.

"Why did you not come forward earlier?" he asked without criticism.

She paused. "Because I am Jewish, and I saw the policeman's cap on Mr. Rybachenko's head. Who would believe a Jewish girl over a policeman? But I did tell my sister, and Sergei...Sergei Khanzhenkov. His father was the chief of police." She hung her head. "Sergei told his father, but he didn't believe him at first."

She lifted her eyes to Goremykin, who began twirling his whiskers. He gazed at the courtroom for some time before he spoke, then he thanked her for coming forward. He told the lawyers that her testimony would be entered as evidence, and asked each lawyer if they had anything or anyone else to present. Neither did. Goremykin fixed his eyes on the senators and instructed them to retire and settle on a verdict.

Rachel trembled as she watched the senators file out. She could see in Goremykin's eyes that he believed her, but she was not sure of the senators at all. As she walked back to her seat, her eyes rested on Mikhail's grandfather. His lips curled up slightly and his eyes softened, as if he was saying thanks to her for standing up and speaking the truth. She saw Mikhail in his weathered face, and she knew that this man, a stranger to her, was a good person like his grandson. Her spirits rose through his silent approval, and for the first time in months she felt genuine hope that things really might get better.

❄❄❄

The senators returned in an hour. Goremykin read the verdict, which found both Mikhail's uncle and cousin guilty, and sentenced them to hard labor—Vasily to ten years and Philip to five. The courtroom was silent as the words sunk in, then it burst into a cacophony of voices that trailed Rachel as she rushed out of court. She was shocked by her own boldness, yet proud of what she had done. She could not bring Mikhail back, but at least she'd made sure the people responsible were punished. Truth had finally conquered evil.

Four

Rachel pulled her shawl tighter around her neck and turned left, toward her old house on Asia Street. She needed to see it one last time before she left Kishinev forever. The roads were still littered with broken doors and windows pushed off to the side, as if they were paying homage to people like her father and Mr. Berlatsky who'd lost their lives in the massacre.

Many businesses were still shut down: a tavern, a bookshop, a hat store, a vegetable market. Rachel wondered what had happened to the owners, and if the shops would ever open again. Fewer people walked along the streets now than before the massacre, and they moved in silence, heads bowed.

The signs of devastation increased as Rachel approached her home. Furniture that had been smashed to pieces lay in piles, abandoned, like so many of the people in the hospital. She stopped when she reached the courtyard of her former house. She touched the cold, stone wall and choked back tears.

A pile of broken tiles lay on the ground, and the courtyard was still strewn with feathers, broken glass, a torn sleeve, and a child's pinafore. The doorway of their house had been boarded up with wood scraps and through the broken windows and twisted frames, there was nothing but darkness.

It looked like a shack, but for Rachel, it held a lifetime of memories—eating Shabbos dinners, playing chess with her father in front of the hot stove, lying on her bench reading, helping her mother prepare meals, arguing with Nucia, then making up. Her previous life flipped through her mind like the pages of a picture book.

As she stared at the remains, she saw something protruding from under a piece of broken glass. Rachel dug away at the spot with a stick until she could see more clearly.

"Father's tallis!" she whispered.

She tore away the debris on top of the prayer shawl until she was able to pull it out. Though no longer white, it was in one piece. Rachel closed her eyes and pictured her father wearing it to the shul. The image settled her and made her feel as if her father was watching over her, Nucia, and her mother.

When she opened her eyes, Rachel felt someone watching her. Turning slowly, she found herself face to face with a tall Russian man, the journalist Korolenko whom she'd seen at the hospital. Rachel stiffened and started to back away from him.

"Have we met?" asked Korolenko, in a robust voice.

"I…I saw you at the hospital."

"Ah, yes, you were reading to some children."

"That's right; what are you doing here?"

"I came to this house to see the damage from the riots that took place during Easter."

Rachel twisted her braid and looked up at him. "Will you tell the truth about what happened, or are you going to spread more lies?"

He peered at her intently before answering. "I always try to tell the truth."

"What if the people you talk to lie? The newspaper here told nothing but horrible lies about us."

"I've seen those articles." His eyes seemed to shine as he spoke. "That's why I'm here. To try and make amends, to set the record straight." He paused. "Would you like to tell me what happened?"

Rachel stared out at the rubble and thought carefully about what to say. "This is where I used to live. I was here when the riots started," she began in a hollow voice. "We hid in the outhouse for hours. All night. One man was killed on the roof as we listened. And my father was killed in the shed."

She cleared her throat and waited for Korolenko to write down what she said. "Mr. Grienschpoun was killed on this spot." Rachel pointed to an area close to where they stood. "He ran past here." Rachel sighed and pointed toward the shed. "He ran past here, and he fell down just there...and that's where they murdered him."

Korolenko stopped writing and stared at Rachel for a moment.

She moved toward the street. "Mr. Nisensen died in a puddle of mud out there." She pointed straight ahead. "A police officer was there the whole time. We thought he'd protect us." She paused. "He didn't."

She was suddenly worn out from describing what had happened. She realized that coming back and reliving the events of that night served no purpose. It was time to go forward, to remember the past but live in the future.

"I…I have to go now," she said. "My mother will be worried."

Korolenko smiled at her. "Thank you for telling me your story."

Rachel shrugged her shoulders. "Do you think that women could be writers like you, someday?"

He smiled at her. "Women are not taken seriously as writers now, but that will change." He paused and gazed into the distance. "If you look outside of Russia, you will see many women attaining fame as writers."

"What are their names?"

"There is Isabella Bird, from England, who writes about places such as Morocco, Japan, Canada, and America. And Emily Brontë, also from England, who wrote the novel *Wuthering Heights* years ago."

Rachel's heart raced as she listened to Korolenko. His words were proof that becoming a writer was not a fantasy, but a very real possibility. Rachel thanked him and turned to go back to the hospital, eager to tell her mother about these women and meeting Korolenko. Still surprised by what he had told her, she looked back to catch one last glimpse of him, but he was gone.

❄❄❄

Sergei traipsed through the empty courtyard and into the hospital. The silence was unnerving

"I'm looking for Rachel Paskar," he said to a woman who was sitting alone in the barren waiting room.

"They've all gone," she said.

"Where?"

"To the train station. We received word that Moldavians are gathered a short distance from here…preparing to beat the Jews." She wiped her eyes with a cloth. "Soldiers are trying to stop them, but after what has already occurred, everyone fled right away. The government has issued hundreds of exit visas so that Jews may escape safely. The only people still here are too ill to travel."

Sergei ran to the door. He raced as fast as he could, past now-familiar landmarks in lower Kishinev…broken-down shops and houses and piles of rubbish at the side of the road, remnants of the Easter riots.

"Menahem," Sergei gasped when he arrived at the orphanage. He was out of breath from running the whole way. "I need to see Menahem now."

"I'm sorry but you can't," said an unfamiliar woman who was blocking the hallway. "It's our Shabbos, you know. None of the children can leave here until this evening after sunset."

"But there won't be an evening for anyone here!" shouted Sergei. "Rioters are on their way right now. You have to take the children somewhere safe—somewhere they won't be a target. I'll take Menahem. I'll make sure nothing happens to him." Sergei's eyes darted behind her, searching for Menahem in the corridor's shadows.

"Why should I trust you?" asked the woman, frowning. "It was your people who started these riots in the first place."

"He is trustworthy," said another voice from the shadows.

Sergei squinted and recognized the woman he had often seen when he came to get Menahem.

"He cares for Menahem," the woman continued, moving toward them. "Menahem will be safe with Sergei."

The other woman cast a sideways glance at Sergei and grunted. "Very well. I'll get the boy." She disappeared down the corridor.

"Sergei!" cried Menahem a moment later. He appeared in the corridor with an excited smile. "Is it true? Are you really taking me away from here?"

"Yes. Now come." Using his hand, he beckoned for Menahem. "We don't have time to talk. I'll explain later." He smiled gratefully at the woman who had vouched for him, grabbed Menahem's wrist, and darted out of the orphanage.

"Where are we going?" asked Menahem.

"On the train. Far from here," puffed Sergei. "Where you'll be safe."

❄❄❄

As she turned back to get one last look at the hospital, a wave of sadness washed over Rachel. She held her journal to her chest, feeling terrible about not being able to say good-bye to Sergei, about not being able to tell him what he meant to her, and how she wished things were different. Though the hospital had been her home for only a couple of months, it seemed like a lifetime. The ties that had bound her to Kishinev for so long had finally been cut. But this hospital had saved them when they had no place else to go, and in its own strange way, it had become her home.

"I wish the Berlatskys were coming with us," she said to her mother and sister as they hurried out of the courtyard. "I'm worried about them."

"You know they can't travel until Chaia is better," said her mother. "There is no other choice." She pushed Rachel forward. "Make haste, Rachel, Nucia…we must get to the station."

As soon as she was on the street, Rachel was immediately swept up and carried along with the crowd scurrying to the train station. The air echoed with children crying and women and men shouting out for them to hurry.

"How are all of us going to fit on the train?" she called out to Nucia. "There must be hundreds of people heading to the station."

"I don't know," said her sister.

Up ahead, Rachel saw the station, a white building with a tall clock tower. As the crowd moved faster, she worried that she would trip and fall and be trampled. She could hear many people weeping and shouting as she and the others were pulled and pushed along.

"Help me!" a woman's voice called out.

"Don't let the train leave without me and my children," cried another.

It was as if a dam had burst. Words rushed through the air, crashing into one another so that they became mixed up and indecipherable. Rachel's head ached as the noise grew. She felt like she was hiding in the outhouse again, that the riots were repeating themselves all around her. That there was no escape.

❄❄❄

"Rachel! Rachel!"

She stopped immediately when she heard Sergei's voice. Rachel peered through the agitated crowd, but couldn't see him.

She shook her head and continued moving forward, craning her neck to catch a glimpse of Sergei.

"Over here, Rachel!"

She turned back in the direction of Sergei's voice, toward the entrance of the station. The arched doorway, framed him with Menahem atop his shoulders. A few stragglers ran past him to catch the train, bumping against Sergei as they rushed by.

"Sergei!" She tried to push against the crowd to get to him, but it was like running uphill on ice.

Nucia screeched at her, "What are you doing? Turn around before you get hurt."

Rachel felt her sister's hand dig into her shoulder, trying to pull her along. "I have to see Sergei…he's here, with Menahem!"

Her mother's voice rose above the crowd. "There's no time! Don't you see? We have to get on the train. It's the last one out tonight, Rachel."

She broke away from her sister's grasp, stuck her elbows out wide, and forced her way through the desperate throng of people, ignoring their dirty looks.

"Sergei…what are you doing here?" she asked when they were close enough to hear one another.

He was breathing hard and moved directly in front of her before responding. "I heard about the riots…I took Menahem…." He set the boy down gently.

Rachel grabbed Sergei's hand and held it tightly. "You've probably saved his life."

As they gazed at each other, the surrounding noise and chaos seemed to fade away. "Come with us," said Rachel. "You said you wanted to travel, to get away from Kishinev. Come with us to America."

Sergei's eyes moved around the station, taking in the madness as people fought their way to the train. "I can't leave my mother and sister, not now, with my father. . . ." He bent down so that his face was at the same level as Menahem's. The boy looked at him with frightened eyes and quivering lips. "You must go with Rachel," said Sergei. "You will be safe with her family."

"No, Sergei, no," cried Menahem. "I want to stay with you." He threw his small arms around Sergei's neck and sobbed on his shoulder.

Rachel, holding back tears, watched Sergei comfort Menahem. *This shouldn't be happening*, she thought. *Menahem shouldn't have to leave Sergei just to be safe. We shouldn't be forced to move from our home, from our country.*

Sergei pried Menahem away from him, and set him on the ground. "I wish you could stay with me, but you need to be with a family that can take care of you." He wiped the tears from Menahem's cheek. "And it isn't safe in Russia for Jews anymore."

"I don't want to be Jewish, I want to be like you," said Menahem.

Rachel watched the color drain from Sergei's face.

"You listen to me, Menahem," Sergei said in a firm voice.

Menahem gazed at him with watery eyes.

"Don't ever change who you are, not for anybody," Sergei continued.

Menahem nodded solemnly.

"Do you think your grandmother would want you to give up everything she taught you, everything your parents knew and believed in?"

Menahem wiped his eyes with the back of his hand and shook his head. His bottom lip quivered but he had stopped crying.

Sergei gently pushed Menahem toward Rachel, who opened her arms for the boy.

Rachel felt Menahem's shoulder blades as she held him tight.

"We have to go, or the train will leave without us," she said, forcing herself to sound in control.

"Write me," said Sergei, handing Rachel a slip of paper with his address. "Let me know when you are out of Russia."

Rachel let go of Menahem, took the paper and stared at it, unable to look at Sergei for fear she would start crying and set Menahem off again.

Sergei reached out and lifted her chin so that their eyes met. "We will see each other again."

"Is that a promise?"

"Yes, and I always keep my promises."

Rachel heard the sincerity in his tone and wanted to melt into his strong arms, to be with him forever, but this was impossible.

"We will see you in Shanghai, or America, and we will be able to be together," she said. "Things will be different, better there."

Sergei nodded, and backed away from them.

Rachel took Menahem's hand. "It will be all right," she assured him as they turned and headed toward the crowd lining the tracks.

"There it is!" Rachel cried when she saw the huge iron train coming toward them. As soon as it stopped, people stuffed themselves into the darkened openings. Arms hung out of the windows, and faces pressed against the glass.

"Rachel...hurry!" cried Nucia.

Rachel saw her sister's face above an open window in the train.

Tightening her grip on Menahem's hand, she ran to the open compartment door nearest to Nucia's window. She lifted Menahem up and then hoisted herself onto the train, relief surging through her as her feet left the ground.

People crammed the train, jostling one another as they fought for room to stand. The train car smelled musty and dirty. Catching the startled eyes of her mother and sister, Rachel smiled wanly, knowing she would have to explain why Menahem was with her. But she also knew that her mother and Nucia would never turn a child away, that they would welcome him and care for him as if he had always been part of their family.

"Am I going to another orphanage?" asked Menahem in a small voice as they huddled together in the aisle.

Rachel put her arm around Menahem's shoulder and held him to her. "I've always wanted a little brother. How would you like to stay with me and my mother and sister?"

He looked up at her, his eyes probing her face, as if he wasn't sure she'd meant what she said. Then, slowly, his lips widened into a smile that warmed Rachel's heart.

As the train gathered speed along the tracks, Rachel looked out the dirty window at the town passing by, a distorted jumble of shapes and images that were hard to recognize as the train accelerated. She couldn't believe they were actually leaving Kishinev, where she had been born, where her father had lived and died, where Chaia still lay, unable to speak, and where she had grown to care for Sergei more than she ever could have imagined.

Rachel thought about him now, her eyes damp with tears. If only Sergei had been able to come with her, if only he had been able to give up his secure world for hers. If only life could be a fairy tale, like the "Snow Maiden," where Ivan gave up everything to live in a castle of ice and be with the woman he loved. Rachel shuddered as she remembered that the love between Ivan and Snegurochka had ended in an instant, when they died together in the warm light of spring.

She looked out the window and saw the river in the distance. It sparkled under the sun, a greenish-brown snake winding its way across the earth. For a second, Rachel thought she saw the reflection of a radiant face with amber eyes and white skin—the face of Snegurochka, the Snow Maiden. She blinked and the image was gone, replaced by a bold ray of sunlight reflecting off the river.

Historical Note

Years will have to go by before the terrible recollection of these doings and of the damning bloodstain on the "conscience of the Christians in Kishineff" can be at all effaced. There is a blot on the consciences not only of those who actually committed murder, but also of those who provoked to murder, by their base lies and their preaching of hatred to their fellow men; and also on the consciences of those who maintain that the fault lay not with the murderers, but with the murdered, that there exist such things as common irresponsibility, and that a whole nation may be treated as having no rights.

—House No. 13, *by Korolenko*

The Kishinev pogrom was a direct consequence of the propaganda of lies and violence that the Russian government pursues with such energy.

—*Leo Tolstoy,* Bulletin annuel de l'AIU 65, 1903

The events of this story are true: fifty-one people were killed, more than four hundred were injured, seven hundred homes and six hundred shops were vandalized or destroyed during the riots in Kishinev. On May 22, 1903, *The New York Times* reported that twenty-five hundred servings were distributed at the soup kitchen daily but that this was but "a drop in the ocean."

Remarkably, the Jews themselves were blamed for the pogrom and were not allowed to meet or gather as a result of this massacre. In the end, twenty-five of thirty-seven rioters were found guilty on various counts and were sentenced to terms ranging from six months to seven years. The stiffest sentences went to two men convicted of murder, who received terms of hard labor for seven and five years. Relations among Jews and gentiles remained strained, and on October 18, 1905, another pogrom took place in Kishinev.

Many of the characters in this book are also based on real people in Kishinev: Ita and Gofsha Paskar, Chaia Berlatsky, Hosea Berlatsky, Sergei's father (Aleksandr Konstantinovich Khanzhenkov), V. G. Korolenko, Lopukhin, Dr. M. B. Slutskii, Bishop Iakov, Rose Katsap (Menahem's grandmother, who was bludgeoned to death while her young grandson looked on in hiding), and Mikhail Rybachenko.

Rachel's life in Kishinev represents the experience of the majority of Jews in this city in 1903. Though they lived in poverty, Jews attended their own schools, which provided instruction in Yiddish and Hebrew. Also, they were able to speak and read Russian, while Russians were unable to communicate in Yiddish or Hebrew.

Mikhail was stabbed to death by a family member for money and his murder led to newspaper stories about Jews killing for blood. These false stories fuelled the 1903 Kishinev Pogrom. I did take the liberty of changing the location of the murder from Dubossary to Kishinev in order to develop more intimate relationships among the characters. I chose the river because the last place Mikhail was seen was skating on a river. Another interesting aside is the fact that Korolenko did meet and talk to a girl at House Number 13, who relayed her version of the pogrom, which he published in *House Number 13*.

Glossary

Balalaika: Triangular-shaped string instrument

Blini: Small pancakes

Bubbe: Grandmother

Challah: Special Shabbat bread loaves

Gorodki: An ancient Russian folk sport where the goal is to knock out groups of pins, which are called cities or towns

Gut: Yiddish for "good"

Gymnazium: School

Hamantashen: A triangular pastry with sweet seed filling

Icon: Tempera pictures of religious scenes and figures that adorned church walls and the eastern walls of family homes. Icon images, based on Byzantine art, were important for Orthodox Russians from birth to death.

Kaddish: A prayer recited by mourners after the death of a close relative

Kopeck: A Russian coin. In 1704, Russia was the first country in the world to introduce a decimal monetary system, where 1 ruble equals 100 kopecks.

Kugel: A baked Jewish pudding made from egg noodles or potatoes, usually served as a side dish on Shabbos

L'chayim: To life—a Jewish toast

Lashon-ha-ra: Speaking the truth about somebody, even though it might be hurtful

Maslenitsa: An eight-day carnival, "Butter Week," where Russians consumed large quantities of blini (small pancakes smothered in butter) at every meal. This fell right before Lent, when butter was prohibited.

Matzah: Unleavened bread eaten by Jews during Passover

Megillah: The Book of Esther, one of the books of the Hebrew Bible. It's the basis for the Jewish celebration of Purim.

Menshe yiden: Good, honest Jewish people

Mikveh: A bath used for ritual immersion in Judaism, to regain purity

Pirozhki: Baked or fried buns stuffed with either fruit, vegetables, or meat

Purim: Commemorates the biblical story of Esther, which marks the deliverance of the Jewish community that lived in Persia

Samovar: A heated container used to boil water for tea and a symbol of Russian generosity

Shabbat, Shabbos: The most important day of the week (Friday) for Jews. It begins eighteen minutes before sunset and ends on Saturday night about forty-five minutes after sunset. During this time, no work or creative pursuits are allowed.

Shiva: The Jewish tradition of publicly mourning the death of a loved one

Sholom Aleichem: Peace be upon you—a greeting from one Jew to another

Shul: A Yiddish word derived from the German word for school, since the shul is a place of learning and a place of prayer

Sobornost: Community

Troika: Carriage or sled drawn by three horses harnessed side-by-side

Verst: Obsolete Russian unit of length defined as 500 sazhen (3,500 feet; 1.0668 kilometers)

Yarmulka: Skullcap worn by men in the shul

Zeyde: Grandfather

Acknowledgments

This book would not exist had it not been for the help and support of many wonderful people: Marsha Skrypuch, for pointing me in the right direction; my agent, Margaret Hart, for reading an early version and providing invaluable comments; Ann Featherstone, for showing me how to fully develop characters; Malcolm Lester, for his insight and keen eye; and Margie Wolfe and Second Story Press, for believing in a new writer.

I'd also like to thank Reverend Dr. Morar Murray-Hayes and Rabbi Stephen Wise for reading the manuscript and providing comments to help ensure its accuracy.

A big thanks to my husband, Steven Greer, and my children, Amanda, Bethany, and Ian, for their enduring patience and encouragement.

About the Author

SHELLY SANDERS has worked as a freelance writer for almost twenty years. Topics she's covered include mental and physical disorders, environmentally friendly design, and real estate trends.

Rachel's Secret was inspired by the life of Shelly's grandmother, a Russian pogrom survivor who fled to Shanghai, and eventually to the U.S. where she received a degree from the University of California at Berkeley.

Shelly lives in Toronto with her husband, three children, two dogs, and two lizards. Visit her online at www.shellysanders.com.